The Enigmatic Coat of Fathers :

An Engineer's Son's Emotional Journal

THE ENIGMATIC COAT OF FATHERS : AN ENGINEER'S SON'S EMOTIONAL JOURNAL

First edition. October 12, 2024.

Copyright © 2024 Yeong Hwan Choi.

ISBN: 979-8224786152

Written by Yeong Hwan Choi.

Table of Contents

The Enigmatic Coat of Fathers

An Engineer's Son's Emotional Journal

Yeong Hwan Choi

<Prologue : Mysterious Email>

2024.09.20 / WEATHER: Cloudy

> Dear Writer Yeonghwan Choi, Hello. I am XXX, an office worker working with your father, Mr. Jeongseop Choi, at the Yeongwol Substation in Gangwon-do.

The sight of my father's name in the very first sentence... My heart skipped a beat and then sank. How long has it been since we last spoke? Months? No, maybe years? His presence wasn't always warm; it was more like a cloud covering the sun. Since becoming an adult, I never once thought about repairing our relationship. I just lived, pretending we didn't exist in each other's lives. And now, news from one of his coworkers had arrived.

> It's about the health of the division chief...

His health? An unfamiliar sense of anxiety slowly seeped through my body. When I was younger, my father was a man with whom emotions were hard to exchange. His world was so different from mine. We had grown so far apart that I lacked the courage to cross that invisible barrier. In the end, we never truly understood each other, and the emotional distance was never bridged. And now, I had to speak about his health "directly"? What could this mean? Had something bigger happened?

> I'm afraid this isn't something to convey in writing, but should be discussed over the phone...

What could be so grave that it couldn't be conveyed in writing? It wasn't just a health issue, was it? A premonition of something more complex crossed my mind. I knew my father had been suffering from diabetes since his mid-30s, but for it to reach a point where it couldn't even be written about... I could feel the unavoidable moment slowly approaching. My hand reached for the phone, and I began slowly pressing in the numbers. Meanwhile, all kinds of scenarios flashed through my mind.

> Please contact me as soon as you see this message.

When was the last time I actually spoke with my father? I couldn't even remember. What could I say if I called? How's everything? Are you feeling okay? Even a simple question like that felt awkward. Though I was aware of his worsening health, there was a lingering fear that I might regret missing out on the last moments. But in the end, I put down the phone without making the call.

The next day, I sat quietly, staring at my Naver inbox. Would I ever be able to make that call? Or was it already too late?

Chapter 1 - Question

2024.09.28 / WEATHER: Clear

The summer had quietly passed, and the world was slowly slipping into the embrace of autumn, known as the "season when the sky is high, and horses grow fat." The once heavy heat under the sun had quietly vanished, and in its place, a calm had settled in. The wind grew lighter, and the sky seemed endlessly high. People either grew accustomed to this change or continued without noticing. The trees proudly flaunted their last remaining colors as if preparing for their grand finale, and leaves began to fall one by one, covering the ground. As evening approached, it was clear that preparing heated mats was necessary; the nights were getting chilly.

I opened my eyes gently as sunlight filtered in and sat down in front of the computer. I stared blankly at the screen with a dull expression. It was 9 a.m. on a Saturday.

Days had passed since I received the email, but my head was still in a fog, and nausea gnawed at me. "What would I feel if my father died?" If he dies, will I be sad? Or would I feel... nothing?

My father was never good at expressing emotions. A friend-like father? Not at all. His tone was always commanding, and he was an absolute presence in the house. His patriarchal authority was almost like an unchanging law. Sometimes, our bottled-up emotions would explode into anger, and those arrows would pierce both our hearts. There was no room for compromise.

Under the guise of discipline, my father sometimes used physical violence as a tool for punishment. Each time his heavy, cruel hand landed on my cheek, the pain pushed me into a state of mental submission. "Why don't you ever listen?" he would yell, but there was no room for explanation or understanding—just silent, violent demands for obedience. Every time, I would hold my breath and wait for the pain to pass. He never felt guilt or regret. "It's for your own good," he would say, a selfish excuse that would often end the violence for the day. He was my father, after all. He was a parent, so of course, he had the right to hit me. That was the logic I grew up with, the unjust selfishness I came to know.

Fathers in the West—when their children climb the stairs, they're quick with a "Good, good, good!" showering praise generously. Their approach to parenting is bright, open, and effusive. But here, in the East, things couldn't be more different.

Particularly between Korean fathers and sons, emotions are seldom displayed. Respect and hierarchy define the relationship, with walls between them as solid as concrete, walls too risky to tear down.

Fathers born in the 1950s were steeped in Confucian values from birth. The family wasn't an emotional haven but a social unit driven by rituals, filial piety, and ranks. A father's role? The steadfast provider. Love and emotional exchange were far down the list, if they appeared at all. To express feelings was considered an indulgence, a luxury no one could afford. Back then, South Korea was growing at an unprecedented pace, and the nation marched towards shared goals with unrelenting focus.

"The Land of Morning Calm"—a mere illusion. Such reverence for order and etiquette? A façade, upheld by the control fathers held over their households.

The distance between father and son often felt as vast as the silence that separated them. But if we were to point out one strength from that generation, it would be resilience, a quiet resolve far stronger than our generation's. They bore storms of emotion deep within and still pressed on, heads held high for the sake of their families.

Simply put, they didn't let emotions lead. Instead, they suppressed them, moving forward in steady silence. It was this unwavering focus that defined the strength of their generation. Our generation prides itself on flexibility and open-mindedness, but we fall short of the stoic perseverance that guided them.

My father, he always wore a mysterious coat to work. It was worn, heavy with age, but perhaps even heavier with the burdens of life he carried.

Every morning, the sound of the door closing behind him would ease the anxiety growing within me, though only for a moment. When evening came, and I heard his returning footsteps, that anxiety would double, filling every corner of the house.

As the front door creaked open, the weight of his coat seemed to smother the room. It became harder to breathe, as if the very air thickened with tension. "Are they going to fight again?" I would ask myself, my stomach tightening with fear. "What's he going to destroy this time?"

The shouting always escalated, and when it did, objects flew. A fan would lift into the air, crash onto the floor, shattering into a mess of metal and plastic. The motor would whine before it sputtered to a stop. The violence wasn't just loud—it was overwhelming, clawing at my senses, leaving my ears ringing long after the fight ended.

Once the anger started, there was no escape. I'd huddle into myself, my heart pounding in rhythm with their escalating voices. I wanted to run, but where could I go? There was no safe place to hide.

I've always been unusually sensitive to sound. When I'm immersed in study or lost in my thoughts, the noises of the house seem to pierce into the deepest corners of my mind. Even the ticking of a clock on the wall can sometimes get under my skin, but the volume of the television—it's like thunder and lightning crashing through the room. The vibrations rip through my brain, tearing apart neurons one by one, as if a hurricane had swept through. To put it simply, "It felt like I was losing my mind."

Yet, even in the midst of this sensory storm, I continue to build my own world, a fragile sanctuary of my own making. Inside it, I am a lonely sailor on a voyage, searching endlessly for some sense of self. And when their arguments erupted, the intensity of the noise became even sharper, more unbearable. I still remember that one day in the kitchen when a knife appeared—those memories remain a deep scar to this day.

In a capitalist society, money is essential. That's a fact no one can deny. I depended on it, my father depended on it, and my mother did too, even though we were tied to a currency as fragile as the won. We valued tangible things over anything intangible, after all, survival demands it.

If money poured out of the ATM endlessly, would my father's existence matter so much? In many ways, my immature understanding of the world was shaped by my mother's character. She was pragmatic, overly so. She was also profoundly negative, constantly suspicious of the future, always trying to cut off any potential uncertainties. Rather than offering hopeful words, her mind was always battling future anxieties, never leaving room for a single gap.

But that kind of approach is futile. Life doesn't work that way—it doesn't flow smoothly just because you've planned everything. Opportunities and crises appear out of nowhere, and our unpredictable fate will always cross paths with the road we're on.

And that kind of relentless control, trying to eliminate every variable, only nurtures more anxiety, bottling up feelings that eventually burst forth. Steve Jobs is an example of this.

After being ousted from Apple in 1985, he found success with Pixar and NeXT, Inc., but his obsession with perfection is still talked about today. He was a man who would control every little detail, suppress every unpredictable outcome, all to achieve the very best result.

When Apple was struggling, even during the creation of the iMac, countless revisions delayed its launch. His team, under constant pressure, could feel the stress of his exacting standards. Apple's fate was hanging by a thread. In the end, the iMac succeeded, but Jobs' perfectionism became another source of tension and anxiety in the process.

The attempt to completely eliminate variables doesn't always lead to positive outcomes. While it may work in success stories, for ordinary people, it stifles creativity and imagination. On top of that, my mother had strong narcissistic tendencies. "Do you know how much I've done for you? I bought you a car, paid for your tuition, gave you everything you needed to live like everyone else. So why aren't you treating me like other kids treat their parents?"

That's how she always was. In her world, everything she did was justified, and if she didn't receive recognition, then clearly, we were the problem.

"Tell me, did I force you to become a government employee? What haven't I done for you? Will writing change anything?" Her words wounded me, yet I realized that behind them, she was hiding her own cowardice. "You just talk, but you don't take action. If you want to succeed, you have to work harder!

After all I've done, you need to show results!" The older she grew, the more erratic her voice became. She didn't love me for who I was; instead, I was merely the proof of her sacrifice, the testament to her success. I was her tool, and she never praised me—not truly. She loved me, yes, but only as a means of validating herself. And in that love, I was always alone.

"Why would you eat the food I made when you don't even listen to me?" My mother's words echoed in my mind, and I could still hear my father's words—"Leave the house if you won't obey"—lingering in the air.

For both of them, threats came as naturally as breathing. "I bought this house with my money," they would say, and if I didn't comply, they'd demand I leave. Once, they even forced a check card into my hands, only to snatch it back in a display of power. When I was younger, it was even more cruel. They stripped me bare, down to my underwear, and pushed me out onto the cold, wind-swept balcony. That shame, that moment, is still carved into my memory, a stain that refuses to wash away.

Why was I even born? I wasn't here to fulfill their desires or meet their expectations. My life was nothing but the product of their biological urges and decisions. But in their worldview, I was always secondary.

As I wrote, a surge of anger began to bubble up inside me. My head grew hot, and I could feel my skin flush as if a boiling liquid coursed beneath it. I bit down on my lip, hard enough to draw blood. "Damn it!" I slammed my fists against the keyboard. Just like my father, I had inherited his temper, and when that fire ignited, it consumed me completely. I didn't want to be like him, but the behaviors I had witnessed all my life were hard to unlearn.

"They say praise makes even a whale dance." No matter how harsh or bitter the world gets, a kind word can change everything. Yet in my family, no such words existed. Only arrows of criticism and judgment flew between us. I was not a whale. I was a stone, sinking deeper and deeper into a sea of unexpressed emotions.

They provided material things, sure—a house, food, a car. But is that all there is? Isn't life about more than just possessions? No matter how expensive the gifts were, they held no value without emotional connection. I was destined to live as an empty shell, a zombie drifting through life, not by accident, but as if it were my fate.

Still, I don't want to blame everything on my parents. My traits and flaws aren't solely their fault. But they undeniably shaped who I am. After all, children are said to be mirrors of their parents.

Especially my mother. Does she ever realize that she might be a narcissist? I doubt it. She doesn't express emotions. It took me a long time to recognize that, but once I did, I stopped trying to talk to her. I just wanted to become that stone.

I live under the same roof with my mother, and at thirty-five, it stings that I'm not financially independent yet. Is this fate too? Yet I know this isn't the end. Someday, no matter how much I've turned to stone, I'll leave this place. Until then, I just have to survive in her narcissistic world without losing myself.

Raised in a household where cold skepticism flowed from my mother and stern patriarchy governed my father, I lived with my emotions tightly bound, locked away. During the endless quarrels between them, it was said that if they ever divorced, I should call my grandmother. In the chaos of fights that often ended with a knife laid back down on the counter, I realized my fate was to confront the tangled, mysterious emotions locked within, like the secrets of Pandora's box.

Yet if there was one common thread between the two, it was undoubtedly their shared financial philosophy. Despite all the visible clashes and turmoil, their approach to money was the bedrock that sustained our family's foundation. The stability of that economic base was unexpectedly solid, even amidst the storm.

South Korea is a country deeply obsessed with comparison. Unlike Europe, where people seem more content with their place in life, Koreans are fixated on rankings. Words like "middle class" and "gold spoon" flood the internet, but to be honest, my family never really fit into that "gold spoon" category. Sure, by internet standards, we might meet the definition, but we lived a simple, ordinary life.

We saved and scrimped. My father never splurged on clothes or shoes, and he wasn't particularly interested in cars either. He drove an Excel, then a Sonata, and eventually a Tucson.

They were the kind of people who understood where money should go and were firm believers in not living extravagantly. Their guiding principle was clear: understand the value of money.

Others might buy new clothes or luxury brands to treat themselves, but my father always wore the same worn, heavy coat. He believed in saving, and any unnecessary purchase was, to him, meaningless. When it came to buying new appliances or furniture, their rule was simple: only when absolutely necessary.

But they weren't stingy. We always ate well, and they took our education seriously. The dinner table was often filled with expensive seafood—plump oysters in season, tender abalone, and fresh prawns. For other families, these might be a rare treat, but for us, they were a regular part of life. We even had premium beef and ribs frequently. But there was a missing piece. We ate well, but we never learned to laugh and share stories over our meals. Eating out meant going to the local tonkatsu joint, and we never experienced the warmth of a cozy restaurant playing classical music. If we could appreciate everything we had, we wouldn't be human. Let's just skip over this part for now.

This was the economic philosophy they passed on to me. Children learn their spending habits from their parents. Growing up, I absorbed their restraint and frugality. Sure, there were times when I wanted to indulge in something luxurious, like the latest gadgets or a designer watch, but I rarely gave in to the temptation. Even after quitting my government job, trying to make a living through writing, and facing several business failures, our family never experienced financial instability. That's because of my father's silent sacrifice. He never gave me warm words or encouragement, but his stoic silence gave me the foundation to stand on. It's something I'm truly grateful for.

Of course, I couldn't rely on that forever. I had to become independent, both financially and mentally. Perhaps this was his way of supporting me—providing financially without showing emotion. It's a lesson I've carried with me throughout my life.

When I think back to the day my father collapsed from his diabetes, the memory is still vivid. I was about six years old, and he was in his mid-thirties. I thought he was healthy, but there he was, being rushed to the hospital. I remember sitting at the far end of the emergency room corridor, staring blankly at the white walls. When I finally reached his room, the sight of all the monitors flashing numbers and his pale face struck me. He was in pain, yet he looked at me with that same, unchanging expression. Maybe that's when I first learned how to hide my feelings—just like him.

Years later, when I became a civil servant, I learned more about his health. When I applied for a leave of absence to study real estate appraisal, I needed to attach his medical records. Meeting with his doctor for the first time, I realized how serious his condition was. The doctor's office was unremarkable, with cold machines and papers scattered everywhere. As I sat down, she began explaining my father's condition. "We're concerned about complications from diabetes," she said, gesturing to her eyes. "If it worsens, his vision will deteriorate." She furrowed her brow slightly and mimicked the narrowing of sight with her fingers. "It's called diabetic retinopathy. It can damage blood vessels, blur vision, and eventually lead to blindness."

She paused and pointed to her feet, leaning forward to indicate the lower extremities. "In extreme cases, we're looking at gangrene, starting with the toes. If circulation is compromised and the nerves are damaged, he might lose sensation and develop infections that won't heal. In the worst case, amputation might be necessary. If not managed, diabetes can damage the heart, kidneys, and nervous system—conditions that accelerate as he ages."

After the serious discussion, our conversation turned casual. She asked about my work, and we talked about real estate appraisal. It was awkward at first, but then her smile softened, and we ended up talking for over an hour. I think she enjoyed talking to a healthy young person, rather than just dealing with patients all day. Strangely enough, I felt more at ease as we talked.

Even with such a serious condition, my father never let us see him falter. If I'm being honest, he wasn't transparent with us. If he had opened up about his vulnerabilities, maybe it could have brought us closer. But that was just as much a part of his nature as the diabetes was.

My father worked at Korea Electric Power Corporation, back when securing a job at a public company meant a lifelong career. He embodied that promise, never letting go of work, even after retirement. Today, in his mid-sixties, with a body long worn down, he continues as a project supervisor in the countryside. I wonder why. With enough savings for retirement, what keeps him tethered to his job? Is it because of me, his unsteady son? Because I quit my stable government job and still haven't found solid ground?

His health is nowhere near good. The last time we heard from the doctors, the prognosis was severe. Yet, each morning, he dons that same old coat and heads out the door, his steps heavier each day. Why won't he stop?

He was undoubtedly an intelligent man. While a university degree doesn't tell the whole story, he graduated from a prestigious university in Seoul, and my mother was no less accomplished. Although I never blindly trusted anyone's opinions or arguments, I recalled a passage from a book on the paradox of intelligence—how the higher the intelligence of parents, the less likely their children are to find happiness. The thought lingered in my mind.

With a soft click of my keyboard, I opened a browser and typed in "high intelligence parents children unhappiness." As I scrolled down, the words leapt out at me, piercing my consciousness as if they were aimed directly at my own situation. The screen filled with statistics and graphs, and I found myself nodding along in silent agreement. It made sense; if parents are too brilliant, their children often feel crushed under the weight of their expectations. My fixation on complex concepts such as philosophy, the universe, and quantum mechanics was not merely a product of curiosity. Deep within me lay an incessant urge to analyze and dissect. According to the MBTI framework, I identify as an INTP—dubbed 'the Architect,' a type known for heightened imagination and creativity, yet notoriously lacking in execution. I can envision countless ideas, yet only a fraction see the light of day. And in areas of keen interest, I dive in with reckless abandon, revealing hints of ADHD tendencies.

Until I learned about the B5 personality framework, the MBTI was the most fitting theory to describe me, even with its inherent contradictions. It wasn't until this concept, born in America long ago, was revisited that I began to understand myself a bit better. Yet, another question arises: Why am I so distant from social success and why does my academic intelligence seem less impressive? I scored between a 3 and 5 on the national college entrance exam, and graduated from the Civil Engineering department at Chungbuk National University. I've worked my way up through a major construction company to a level 7 civil servant, but I've never considered my life to be particularly remarkable. If I had to pinpoint my peak, it would be my university grades, where I was considered part of the upper tier. It was a time when fascinating subjects drew me in, and studying was genuinely enjoyable. Outside of that period, why have I found it so difficult to approach success, despite facing so many possibilities?

In contrast, my younger sister is a different story. She embodies all the criteria for success in South Korea, having graduated at the top of her class from Seoul National University's dental school, and now confidently practices as a doctor. There's a three-year age gap between us, yet we rarely crossed paths during our upbringing. While I was a high school student, she entered Sangsan High School; by the time I was serving in the military, she was attending university in Seoul. Our lives during those years were entirely different.

I don't necessarily believe that graduating from Seoul National guarantees high intelligence. Perhaps I inherited some of that intelligence from somewhere, but it seems I'm merely floundering in philosophical exploration, chasing ideals instead. My time as a civil servant was fraught with challenges, particularly within that conservative environment. As I became increasingly aware of my differences from others, my place there became more precarious, shaping the person I am today. Even while belonging to the ranks of civil servants, I always found myself gazing out towards the vast world beyond.

The conversation has strayed for a moment. If we set aside the issue of parental intelligence, what then is the root of this awkwardness? Why have we lived so indifferently toward one another? While it's true that we are entangled in the threads of cultural, historical, genetic, and temperamental legacies, I can't help but ponder the influence of biological characteristics as well. It might be unfair to interpret my father's every behavior solely through the lens of masculinity, but undeniable facts remain. Men are not accustomed to expressing emotions.

Beyond social and cultural environments lies a biological structure, complete with its hidden complexities. Numerous studies suggest that men feel emotions less frequently than women do, rooted in their XY chromosomes. This particular pair of chromosomes, alongside the male hormone testosterone, is associated with traits like aggression, competitiveness, and focus. Unlike estrogen, which enhances the ability to perceive and express emotions, these traits prioritize efficiency and logic. Typically, women are more adept at fostering emotional exchanges and empathy, often comfortable in expressing their feelings. The differences between the XX and XY chromosomes extend not only to how one perceives the world but also to how one reacts emotionally.

Could it be that his feelings were conceived and ultimately lost within the confines of those chromosomes? The subtle distinctions between XX and XY are not merely academic; they manifest in how we engage with our feelings and interpret our experiences. Is this merely a characteristic of male biology, or is it a construct of the false "masculinity" shaped by cultural and temporal influences? It is clear that I cannot expect warmth or connection from my father. And I am not alone in this feeling, am I? I am convinced that over fifty percent of sons in this age share similar sentiments. There's an icy distance—an inability to express emotions, and the chasms between us remain unfilled. Was it my failure to reach out to my father that created this void, or was it that he could never step forward toward me? His authority and presence linger behind me like a dark shadow, always

there, yet ever intangible.

Yet, on rare occasions, our conversations unfolded in unexpected length. On one of those rare days when my typically reticent father opened up with an unusually long dialogue, instead of feeling lighter, the weight of his words pressed down upon me even more. He still struggled to understand me, and I found myself equally lost in his perspectives. The advice he offered, which might seem altruistic at a glance, constricted my throat and blurred my vision.

"How can you achieve anything without a goal? You always do this," he admonished, and that one phrase cast me into silence. I recalled the tone of his voice, his inflection, and the expression he wore at that moment. After that awkward exchange had concluded, I entered my room and sank heavily into my chair, where unfinished drafts lay scattered across my desk.

'Will I fail again? Will I once more feel that my father's words ring true?' My grip tightened around the pencil.

In the East, steeped in Confucian ideals, I often found myself envious of fathers who had the camaraderie of friendship with their sons. During my school years, I watched as they climbed mountains together on weekends, their laughter echoing in the steamy air of saunas, sharing the minutiae of daily life and their struggles. Those moments of joy seemed a distant dream, one I longed to grasp yet could never quite touch.

"The grass is always greener on the other side," isn't it? It's a sentiment that rings true. Yet, it's important to acknowledge that there have certainly been Eastern fathers who, like their Western counterparts, exude a sense of freedom and lightness. As a child, I often imagined those fathers effortlessly sharing their worries and feelings.

Reflecting on previous anecdotes, my mother, despite possessing the XX chromosomes, was highly critical and extremely poor at expressing emotions. Growing up in that environment, I became someone who struggled to understand others' feelings, dulled to the very notion of emotion itself. Just as the proverb goes, "You reap what you sow," the reflection of parents is often found in their children. I too grew up with many traits mirroring my father. There are moments when buried feelings swell inside me, reaching a point where they can no longer be contained, and suddenly, they explode. While I may appear emotionally numb most of the time, I realize that this is merely a facade I've constructed to suppress those feelings.

The monster of emotion that erupts after years of repression is another side of me, cast in the shadow of my father. However, this doesn't mean that I lack sensitivity. To elaborate a bit further, emotion and sensitivity are quite distinct.

If emotions are the waves that momentarily shake the heart, then sensitivity is like the breeze dancing atop those waves. While others may shed tears at sad lyrics, I find greater solace in melodies that flow through me without words. The gentle resonance of a piano, the vibrations of string instruments—these are the elements that free my spirit. And then there's the art gallery.

Every time I step in to view the paintings, the fragments of my sensitivity come alive. While people comment on a piece, saying, "This is sad," or "That is joyous," I tend to imprint the soul of the artist onto my heart more than I dwell on those emotions. Each brushstroke holds a subtle tremor, each color a delicate contrast.

Is it a defense mechanism I'm trying to construct? The fear of being swept away by the waves of emotions that might crash upon me after someone dies? Suddenly, I'm reminded of my beloved dogs, 'Haeng-un' and 'Hee-mang,' who ascended to the heavens. It was a sunny Saturday in the spring of my sophomore year in middle school, 15 years old. My mother and sister brought home a fluffy cotton candy from a local family. As time passed, I met another sweet fluffball, 'Haeng-un,' during my college days, and soon after, while serving in the military and finally landing a job as a civil servant. When that familiar flavor of cotton candy came back to me at 12 years old, a new, sweet cotton candy graced our home, bringing with it a unique blend of flavors. Those days spent with my two angels became my most cherished memories. The long-standing sweetness of cotton candy encompassed my entire growth journey, and the love I received from those little creatures was beyond any words I could muster.

However, the unexpected moment of parting arrived, bringing with it an unbearable sadness. After Haeng-un departed at the tender age of 17, just two years later, my second cotton candy faded from view at just 7 years old. Unlike humans, animals live by recognizing and understanding each other's differences. They offer us nothing but pure love and loyalty. It's unfortunate that the phrase 'worse than a dog' is often used to demean others. Yet, in reality, we humans harbor countless flaws compared to these endlessly loving and loyal creatures. We are often duplicitous, betraying each other, acting selfishly, and are embarrassingly petty.

The saying "When the hen crows, the household falls apart" has transformed into "If you listen to women, you'll find rice cakes even while you sleep." We might need to reflect on that expression once again.

I grasp my pen, reminiscing about those days and letting my thoughts spill onto the page.

- My Beloved Cotton Candies -

Maltese 'Hee-mang' is a tart cotton candy, while 'Haeng-un' embodies the sweetness of pure confection. This delightful blend of flavors never fades. The tantalizing aroma transports me back to my childhood, and each thought of them revives that special scent. Their tart sweetness brought me happiness, and their warm affection and innocence filled my heart with joy. Every time their tiny tongues would lick my face, I could taste their love. The crinkling of cotton candy whispered sweet nothings into my ears. Their pattering footsteps graced my daily life with little blessings. Although the cotton candy melts away quickly on my tongue, those sweet and sour memories remain vivid in my mind. Likewise, their love and memories never truly dissolve; they continue to dance within my senses.

In this room, the echoes of their breaths gently caressed me, if only for a moment. Reflecting on it, I realize that when they departed for the heavens, I suppressed those feelings of farewell, just as I do now. I loved them dearly, and the memories we created together were filled with pure happiness, yet I still struggle to confront those genuine emotions. Am I trying to turn a blind eye? Or is it that I loved them so deeply that I can't bear the weight of the sorrow that comes with their loss? Perhaps I long for a numbness that shields me from the pain.

It's a fallacy to think that just because we're family, we truly know each other. We may occupy the same space daily, sitting at the same table and forcing down meals together, but that doesn't mean we genuinely understand one another. My father and I have always operated this way. Each time we meet, we exchange only superficial pleasantries. He would issue commands, and my responses were limited to complying with those orders. The idea of sharing feelings was a fantasy, one I never even dared to dream about. Perhaps that's why I realize I know nothing about him. I can't fathom what thoughts have shaped his life or what emotions have sustained him through the years. Is this a unique issue to our family, or is it a common plight for all families? Is it natural that, despite spending so much time together, we remain strangers? Are we living in the illusion that simply being in each other's presence obligates us to understand one another?

The absence of communication has been a deep-rooted decay, nestled firmly in the foundations of our family. From a young age, my father and I never truly engaged in meaningful conversation. Perhaps that's why I've always felt a sense of emptiness. Though family surrounds me, I believe they can never truly grasp my essence. We confront each other daily, yet remain oblivious to one another's inner lives. Even now, as I sense my father's impending death, I find myself unable to comprehend him. And I know he cannot understand me either. After all, he was the one who often remarked, "That's just your perspective."

Moreover, I find myself confused about even the coat he wore daily to work. Was it a deep brown, or was it a faded gray? Each evening, when I sense the heavy presence of that coat hanging in the hallway, I can't help but wonder if it concealed something significant within its folds.

The coat was, quite literally, suspicious. It was neither merely worn nor faded; it bore a weight that felt simultaneously heavy and light. I often found it difficult to gauge its true heft. It symbolized the unbridgeable distance that existed between my father and me—superficially shallow and airy, yet shrouded beneath it was a profound shadow of indifference. This multitude of emotional distance accumulated layer upon layer.

That weight mirrored the wall constructed from our silence. We were unable to surmount that barrier, and as a result, we could not easily unpack the weight of each other's lives. The reason why that coat always sprang to mind when I thought of my father was perhaps because I had grown more accustomed to its symbolism than to its tangible essence. And if he were to vanish from this world, I might find myself unraveling the secrets he left behind, possibly gaining some sort of understanding in the process.

Putting aside the chaotic emotions of the past, I moved the mouse to open an internet window and began to type. > Search term: What emotions do people feel?

Countless blogs, psychological research papers, some questionable articles, and heated discussions spilling thoughts in community forums appeared on the screen. I clicked on one at random and began to scroll slowly. "Human emotions can be classified into 27 categories." "There are six basic emotions; the rest are more nuanced." "Each emotion can manifest in various ways depending on the situation," various snippets of information flashed before me. Happiness, anger, sadness, fear, disgust—the chart displayed these feelings in an orderly array. Twenty-seven emotions, and beyond that, even more intricate sub-emotions.

The diagrams kindly detailed the interrelationships of each emotion. Anger intertwined with fear, sadness connected to emptiness, and loneliness aligned side by side with anxiety

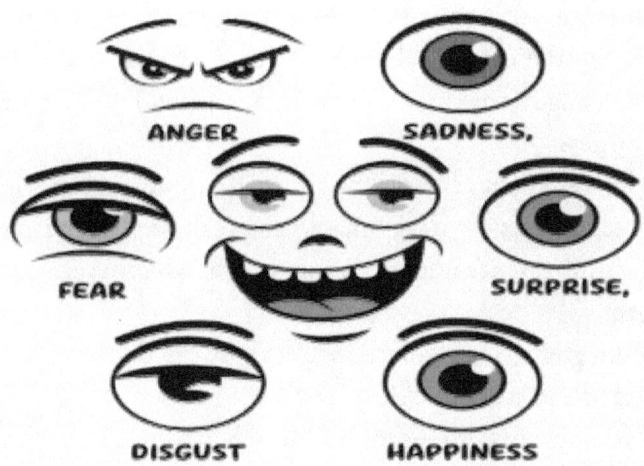

ANXIETY

It is said that the first emotion that washes over a person at the moment of death is anxiety—the vague fear that lingers in the face of mortality. As I ponder this word, I wonder if such anxiety lurks deep within my heart. When I imagine my father's death, do I feel terrified? Or am I simply numb? It's hard to tell.

Loneliness

If my father were to pass away, would I feel loneliness? Our relationship lacked warmth or affection, so his absence doesn't seem likely to evoke that sense of isolation. Yet, is it possible that an unrecognized depth of loneliness exists within me? As someone who struggles with emotions, I can't pinpoint this certainty.

Sadness

Even though I knew my father was suffering from diabetes, I have never truly mourned for him. I simply let those moments slip away, indifferent.

Anger

Perhaps I might feel anger towards my father. His strictness, his cold demeanor—love was something I couldn't perceive from him. Reflecting on the emotional voids I've experienced because of him, I suspect that anger may run deeper within me than I've imagined.

Emptiness

Emptiness. What remains for me when my father is gone? Likely, nothing at all. I find myself unable to recall any shared memories. Ultimately, his absence might carry no weight whatsoever.

Regret

Will I regret the unresolved matters between us, the conversations left unsaid, the irretrievable time?

As I read through the emotions I searched for—anxiety, loneliness, sadness, anger, emptiness, regret—each enveloped me, yet none approached clearly. It felt as if I were standing still in a thick fog. While trying to organize these feelings, I imagined the emotions I might encounter in the face of my father's death. The more I envisioned, the more tangled the feelings became. I set down the mouse and leaned back in my chair, closing my eyes. Sadness? Loneliness? Or perhaps fear? Each emotion approached me as if whispering its name.

Q. If emotions could flow like time, which ones would drift slowly, and which would fade away swiftly?

Q. If we could express a person's heart as a mathematical equation, would my sadness be a complex polynomial filled with unknowns, or a simple linear function?

Q. If emotions could be visualized, what colors or shapes would they take? Would my anger dissipate like a cloud, or would it surround me like a solid wall?

Longing

At first glance, it seemed that longing could not possibly exist within the relationship between my father and me. It felt like an emotion that simply did not belong. After much contemplation, I chose five words from the multitude of emotions that might encapsulate what I would feel after my father's death. I wanted to visualize my feelings and quantify them with my own formula. If emotions could manifest as numbers and graphs before my eyes, I believed I could accurately pinpoint my position even amid the impending storm. I had faith that such clarity would allow me to measure the depths of my emotions without being swept away by the tide. Perhaps controlling the vast, indistinct depths of the ocean's darkness was my final line of defense.

I gently set aside the inquiry email I received about my father and made my way to bed. It was 1 PM. My body, nestled under the covers, swayed back and forth like a flag on a small boat adrift in a sea where the winds would pass through it sporadically. I hoped that closing my eyes would help distance me from the tangled thoughts swirling within, but discomfort quickly bubbled to the surface. My body grew languid, yet the unease in the corner of my mind would not release its grip on me. Thus, as evening approached, I found myself in a loop of rising and sitting back down, wasting the entire day in restless contemplation.

Chapter 2: Pain

2024.09.29. / WEATHER: Clear

The following Sunday, silence flowed effortlessly, as if it belonged to nature itself. As I drifted into daydreams, I found emotions to be little more than illusions. Humans, in their desire to communicate these intangible feelings, had chosen to crystallize them into words. Anxiety, sorrow, anger—mere labels devoid of tangible substance. These emotions, symbols representing our internal states, exist solely to facilitate communication among people!

My stomach began to grumble softly. I ambled into the kitchen, pondering what to eat. My gaze fell upon a lone lemon, its vibrant yellow beckoning me. I lifted a glistening knife, its cold steel blade sending a shiver through my fingertips. As I brought it down, the sharp edge grazed the fruit's surface, sending a slight tremor through my palm. The lemon's skin was firm, yet it yielded easily as the blade pierced through, revealing a rich, deep yellow beneath its thin, rough exterior. With each slice, a zesty aroma filled the air.

As I cut the lemon precisely in half, juice burst forth, accompanied by a sharp, tangy scent that intensified around me. I took a bite from one half, its distinct acidity making me squint slightly as the flavor exploded across my palate, the juice trickling down to my lips and, almost instantly, coursing through my senses, igniting a myriad of sensations in my mind.

The sharpness and freshness, the cold blade, the juice that spilled forth—could emotions not be similar? If these intangible feelings could transform so concretely into sensory experiences, I believed I could grasp and measure them more clearly. Lost in my thoughts, I inadvertently pressed the knife's tip against my thumb. A mere touch, yet it broke the skin, leaving a thin line from which pain immediately radiated throughout my body. As blood began to surface, forming a small crimson bead, the word "pain" silently surfaced from somewhere deep within me.

"Ah... Damn. That hurts."

Pain always arrives unexpectedly, initially appearing as a trivial scratch, yet hiding within it something larger and more intricate. The first word that springs to mind from that pain is "Pain" itself—a word bearing a weight beyond mere sensation.

I reflect on this small wound and my relationship with my father. The punishments he dealt and the strictness he exhibited, along with the harsh exchanges we shared, have cut into me like that blade.

"Is pain an emotion, or is it a sensation?" Why do people label this discomfort as "pain" at times, and "ache" at others? Even as I watch blood slowly bead on my thumb, my thoughts spiral onward. If pain is a sensation, then it would be an immediate reaction to external stimuli, much like the sharp zest of a lemon.

However, the way individuals process that pain varies widely. Could it be that pain is rooted not in sensation but in emotion? Regardless, I find myself contemplating how this one word encapsulates the entirety of human suffering.

● Anxiety, sorrow, anger: these three emotions are merely different names for pain. Pain is the collective essence that embraces them all. Like drawing a set in mathematics, I began to envision circles in my mind. At the center, of course, sat the word "Pain," surrounded by three smaller circles. They were interconnected yet each possessed distinct characteristics.

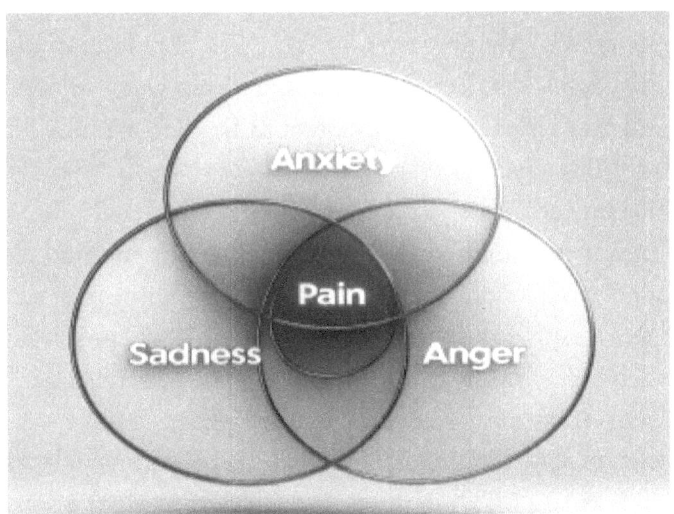

ANXIETY, MORE SENSITIVE than anything else, is a bundle of tension that can erupt at any moment, and within its junction lies always an undercurrent of sadness. It's a serene yet profound feeling, as unfathomable as a bottomless well.

For a long time, emotions rooted in deficiency— the love I never felt from my father and the childhood I lived without expectation— settled in my heart.

'Pain':I envision these three emotions revolving together within a single circle. When I conceptualize them as a set, the intertwined feelings become complex yet simultaneously clear. The process of drawing my own formula in shapes may well be a constant struggle against intangible emotions. While they remain invisible to the eye, they undoubtedly exist, and I grapple with defining them through numbers and lines. If those emotions are ultimately illusions, then I also have the right to construct a virtual reality that freely expresses those feelings.

Meanwhile, the hastily wrapped bandage still clings to my throbbing thumb, dangling from my skin. The thin layer of ointment might absorb, but the deeper pain lurking within seems impervious to any remedy. As I ponder the emotion of pain, a fleeting thought of my father drifts into my mind.

"What university are you aiming for?"

To be honest, I didn't have a specific university in mind. But that explanation never resonated with my father. He always insisted that I needed to have goals and plans. "Without goals, how can you get into a top-tier school? Words may head to Jeju, but you have to land in Seoul."

"Is studying everything? Why can't I pursue what I want?"

The fervor for education in South Korea borders on madness. High school ends at 10 PM. From there, students head straight to academies or sit in study rooms, clinging to their books until 2 AM. In the deepening darkness, when children in other countries are fast asleep, Korean students grip their pencils under the glow of bright lights. The only sounds that pierce the night are the scratching of pens against paper and the sighs mixed with muffled groans.

Our education system is a massive apparatus, cloaked in the guise of "study," driven by intense competition. To survive in this age of infinite rivalry, sacrifices are inevitable. Staying up all night has become the norm, and weekend breaks are a luxury. In the eyes of parents, only grades matter; they believe that grades are the keys to their children's futures. Everyone is sprinting in the same direction, eyes fixed on the same goal.

The generation of my parents experienced firsthand the rapid growth of South Korea. As they climbed the steep stairs of economic success, they learned what it meant to thrive. To them, a university degree was the hallmark of success. "You must attend a good university to land a good job, and only by entering a professional field can you gain a competitive edge over others. There is no easier path to success than through studying," was an unwavering truth. Even after enduring the uncertainties of the IMF crisis and the heights of growth, a university's name became both a shield and a weapon for them. The fear that without this shield, one could not survive the battlefield of life engulfed the entire nation. A single line on a report card or the name of a university could dictate the course of one's life in this society.

I replied tersely, "Understood." Damn, why must their words always be right? They never asked for my opinion. The words of adults were always regarded as "the best path," and I was merely a follower. Within the household, hierarchy dictated superiority, and my father's authority was absolute. In the East, Confucianism takes authority for granted, and as one ages, the hierarchy becomes increasingly clear.

Then came the last day before the college entrance exam. That night, I planned to go to church with my mom. I felt the need to gather my thoughts or perhaps say a prayer asking for a miracle on the exam. As I reached for the front door, my father exclaimed, "What church are you going to the night before the exam? Do you think praying will raise your scores? Just study!"

Anger surged within me. "I'm going to do it my way!" In that instant, my father's face hardened. He grabbed me by the collar. "How did I raise you? Is this how you act?" His voice trembled. I closed my eyes, wishing fervently for the moment to pass.

What if he had been a Western father? Perhaps he would have conversed with me like a friend, discussing various topics. "Trying to do things your way isn't such a bad idea," he might have said, seeking to understand me. They prioritize dialogue with their children, making efforts to recognize their differences. However, Eastern fathers tend to suppress emotions and maintain their positions by exerting authority over their children.

If Latin in Rome is the root of European culture, then the roots of the East lie in the realm of Chinese characters and Confucianism. This authority is not just a personal characteristic of the father but a product of values passed down over thousands of years. Particularly in

Korea, this Confucian culture has taken root more strongly than in any other country. Until the early 2000s, the rates of Confucian inheritance were 61% in Korea, 23% in Japan, and 16% in China. This is largely because Japan and China have attempted to uproot Confucian thought through the Meiji Restoration and the Cultural Revolution, respectively.

The place where this authority is most visibly expressed is at the kitchen table. A meal can only begin once the father picks up his spoon, while the children must wait quietly. If anyone dares to serve themselves first, a reprimand follows: "What gives you the right to pick up your spoon first?" This statement transforms the act of dining from merely satisfying hunger into a ritual of affirming the father's authority. Eating is not just an instinctual act of hunger but a vital etiquette that maintains the hierarchy and order of the household.

The same applies when drinking alcohol. Of course, my father and I have never had a drink alone together. In Korea, when a subordinate pours a drink for a superior, they must hold the cup with both hands. One cannot lift a cup or bottle with one hand in front of an elder, and when drinking, one must turn their head away.

These etiquettes are not mere social niceties; they define familial relationships and create walls. Emotions between parents and children become suppressed, and communication vanishes. While respect and etiquette may represent order, that order contributes more to building walls, like the Great Wall of China, than to fostering understanding. I have never felt a sense of 'comfort' from my father. Our conversations have always been interrupted, and his gaze has always been filled with demands.

In this context, I could understand why a book titled "Confucius Must Die for the Country to Live" was published. The Confucian order established by Confucius may have been necessary in its time, but today it feels disconnected from our philosophy. "This is the path for you. Do this. Do that."

Was that path truly meant for me? Or was it merely the route my father deemed optimal for me?

Today, I find myself drawn into reflections on the past, holding tightly to wounds that cannot be healed with ointment. No matter how hard I struggle, I witness my fading self within this pain from which I cannot escape.

2024.09.30. / Weather: Clear

The next day, at 11 a.m., I naturally opened my eyes. After leaving my civil service job, I now woke up later than most, living the life of a writer and freelancer. Stretching my arms high, I welcomed the day at a leisurely pace and made my way to my favorite café nearby. This fleeting moment felt incredibly sensitive and complex. If I were even a little late, the civil servants from the government office and city hall would swarm out like ants, making the streets bustling with activity during lunchtime. Inside the café, the crowd was thick, and I expected my coffee to arrive quickly, but it took quite a while to finally grasp a cup in my hands.

I hurried my steps. Upon arrival, I ordered an Americano, savoring the aroma of the coffee as I slowly took a stroll around the neighborhood. The first sip of coffee slid down my throat, leaving a lingering bitterness on my tongue. Koreans often describe this taste as "bitter-sweet."

"Isn't bitterness a form of pain?"

As the bitter flavor spread across my palate, enduring a slight discomfort felt too trivial to label as suffering. However, if I were to add another cup of espresso—or no, maybe two, three, or even ten shots—the intensity of that bitterness would heighten. "Then perhaps I can measure the intensity of pain through coffee?""What if I drank 100 shots of espresso? How would the intensity change? Wouldn't a direct proportional function that numbs the taste buds reveal itself before my eyes?"

The more it increases, the more unbearable that intangible element becomes—"Pain."

If I could categorize pain in stages, just as I adjust the strength of coffee, then the impact on my heart would also vary according to its intensity. After my walk, I returned home and headed to the kitchen. The savory aroma wafting from the toaster filled the air, teasing my nose. I pulled out a perfectly toasted slice of bread, thickly slathered it with warm, melting butter, and topped it with fresh jam. As I took a bite, the crispy texture combined with the sweet and nutty flavors spread across my mouth. This moment, awakening both my sense of smell and taste, filled me with energy.

Eventually, I sat down at my computer and flipped through a notebook stained with sketches. I picked up a pencil that had been lying around on the corner of my desk, and the familiar sound of the pencil scratching against the paper filled the air.

"If my father were to die, could I quantify my emotions in a formula?""And if I could categorize the intensity, wouldn't I be able to anticipate how high the waves of those emotions would crash over me?"

Sigh... But wait, I need data. "Of course, I don't have the data!"I needed numbers based on experience. I set the pencil down and shook my head.

"See, my mind isn't that sharp. Suck!"

2024.10.02. / Weather: Cloudy then Clear

Two days later, I began the experiment to measure pain. As usual, I ordered a cup of espresso. The first cup was, unsurprisingly, calm. The bitter aroma and taste stimulated my nose and tongue, awakening my senses. It hardly felt like pain; if anything, it was closer to pleasure.

Once home, I prepared my coffee pot, shaking out the remnants from yesterday and adding freshly ground beans. Then I poured in the water. One cup, two cups... ten cups. The bitterness of caffeine pressed down on my tongue, and my heart began to race. Nine cups, ten cups. When I reached my limit, an irregular heartbeat surged through me, and it felt as though my body was burning up. With each sip, my stomach twisted. It felt like someone's thick, heavy hand was squeezing my chest.

As caffeine seeped into my system, anxiety began to rise. Suddenly, I glanced at my arm and pinched my skin with my fingers. Just a light tease of discomfort. I pinched again, this time harder.

Pain sent a sharp signal right away. The sensation in my arm became clearer, and the more I increased the pressure, the more pronounced and vivid the pain coursed through my nerves. I kept pinching my arm, documenting the intensity, focusing intently on understanding the linear pattern of rising pain. Suddenly, a memory from a past car accident came rushing back.

Years ago, an unexpected accident at an intersection. The sudden, violent twist inside the car led to a herniated disc in my back. That pain returned. Whenever I bent over, the heavy ache between my bones surged. Every long moment spent seated intensified the pain, pressing deeper and sharper into my lower back.

2024.10.03. / Weather: Rain

The next day began tolerably. As the first sip of espresso slid down my throat, the bitterness stirred a sharp pain in my body momentarily. But it was okay. I was used to this level of bitterness. The discomfort I felt pinching my thigh was also a familiar one.

As the second and third cups passed, a devil's drumbeat echoed in my heart. One beat, two beats, three beats...

My breath grew shorter, labored, each gasp tearing through the air. There was not enough oxygen. It felt as if my lungs had failed, and my body began to sway. My legs weakened, my hands and feet trembled, and nausea rose within me. The bitter aroma of the espresso transformed into a revolting aftertaste, burrowing deep into my gut.

"Ugh!"

As the pain wrapped tighter around me, a rough sound clawed at my throat, escaping into the air. Cold sweat beaded on my forehead, and droplets trickled down my neck. In an instant, I felt a rush of heat, only for my body to grow cold once more. A chill pressed against my skin, and the shivering intensified, trembling like a aspen tree. My pupils darted uncontrollably from side to side, the world around me blurred. Tears welled up in my eyes, spilling down my cheeks.

After resting for about three hours, I resumed the routine of gathering different data. Sitting at my desk for hours, the pain from my herniated disc escalated. My hand, gripping the pen, began to tremble, and that pain spread from my lower back up through my spine, radiating throughout my body. I closed my eyes, took a moment to catch my breath, and quantified the intensity of the pain for myself.

"Right now, it's about a 5... no, maybe a 6."

I tried to rise from the desk, but my legs gave way, and I collapsed to the floor. Reluctantly, I dragged myself to the bed and pressed an ice pack against my back. The cold sensation gradually enveloped the pain in my lower back, and I recorded this moment—the process of pain diminishing from an 8 to a 6.

As my body felt a bit better, I began another experiment, this time pinching my arms while lying on the bed. I started gently. "1, that's manageable." Gradually, I increased the intensity. With each pinch of my nails digging into my skin, I noted the pain levels: 3, 4, 5... The deeper and more intense the pinches became, the more that pain etched itself into my body. Before long, the skin on both arms was turning a deeper shade of red. The places my fingers touched glowed as if a rubber band had been pulled and released, deepening over time until they darkened. Tiny capillaries burst, and a shallow ache erupted, crying out for attention. The area near the veins swelled slightly, and the skin tightened, the boundaries of the bruise becoming distinct. Even the slightest movement of my arms sent a heavy pain radiating through me.

A day later, the bruises on my arms had deepened further. Both arms had swelled from a bluish hue to a dark red. When I tentatively slid my sore arm beneath my sleeve, the sting was nearly unbearable. "Now it's at a 9... almost at its limit."

This is Pain.

This suffering, more a vast entity than an emotion, has become my constant companion. Each morning, I incrementally increase my coffee intake, meticulously documenting how my body responds, quantifying the intensifying discomfort from my herniated disc. I pinch my arms and thighs, measuring the degree of pain step by step.

Though each sensation possesses its own intensity and quality, their essence converges into a singular experience

.

Pain Formula

$$Pain(x) = \alpha C^2 + \beta P^2 + \gamma D$$

Where:

C: Number of shots of coffee consumed

P: Intensity of pain when pinching the arm

D: Pain from a herniated disc

α, β, and γ are constants that vary depending on the experimental conditions.

To explain this formula, my unique pain intensity is determined by three intertwined factors. The first factor is the pain that arises from the bitterness of coffee.

As the number of espresso shots increases, the corresponding physiological reactions escalate exponentially, which I denote as C2. This bitterness does not merely linger in my mouth; it stimulates my entire nervous system, amplifying my discomfort.

The second factor is the pain I experience when I pinch my arms. This pain spikes dramatically depending on the intensity of the pinch, which I label as p3. The stronger the pinch, the greater the surge in pain. Finally, the pain from my herniated disc strikes with immediate, jarring force; thus, I treat it linearly. This pain consistently torments me, maintaining a fairly constant level of severity and frequency, which I represent as D.

Segmentation of Pain (Anger, Anxiety, Sorrow)

I have precisely quantified what these three emotions signify. To understand how each of these emotions inflicts pain upon me, I derived the following formulas.

Anxietyresembles a smoldering ember, gradually taking root in my mind. It is often triggered by unpredictable situations, injecting tension into my psyche.

· **Anxiety** $= \delta A + \varepsilon U$

A : Average intensity of anxiety experienced in a day

U : Amplification of pain in unpredictable situations

δ , ϵ : Constants that vary by individual; the higher the unpredictability, the exponentially greater the intensity of anxiety.

Sorrowis like the deepening depths of a tranquil sea. As tumultuous waves crash through, the ensuing stillness delivers an even more profound pain.

· **Sorrow** $= \mu S + \nu$

S : Intensity of emotional shock

μ , ν \mu, \nu μ , ν : Constants that vary according to psychological state.

Angerresembles a volcano on the brink of eruption. It reacts instantly to stimuli, surging violently, and when self-control falters, its force becomes even more potent.

· **Anger $= \xi \mathbf{F}^2 - \eta \mathbf{R} / \mathbf{F}$**

F : Intensity of the stimulus that provokes anger

R : The strength that suppresses anger

ξ, η : Correlations between anger sensitivity and suppression.

Thus, the overall formula for pain can be expressed as:

∴ **Pain = Anxiety + Sorrow + Anger**

2024.10.20. / Weather: Rain

As I gazed at the notebook lying on my desk, the entries from the past few weeks filled the space with a silent intensity. These figures, which had weighed down on me, encapsulated the anxiety, sorrow, and anger I had experienced. Now it was time to validate them. I needed to determine what the accumulated data meant and whether the pain I felt could truly be defined by these three emotions.

I wondered if the numbers I had recorded while pinching myself, collapsing onto the floor, and enduring the pain of my herniated disc represented the pain I discovered within my relationship with my father.

Before I could verify this, I took a moment to reflect. The sorrow I sensed in my father's tone and expression stemmed from the gap between his expectations of me and my inability to fulfill them, didn't it? That sorrow resonated within me, quietly suffocating me, gradually solidifying into a singular, repressed emotion over time.

Was the pain I felt genuinely a product of my relationship with my father? Anxiety, sorrow, and anger—these three emotions might well be the legacy he left behind for me.

The Tools of Anxiety

I decided I needed to buy a heart rate monitor. I clicked on Microsoft Edge and opened Google. As soon as I typed the words into the search bar, a plethora of products flooded the screen. With a quick click, I found myself on Amazon, where prices varied wildly, and features differed significantly.

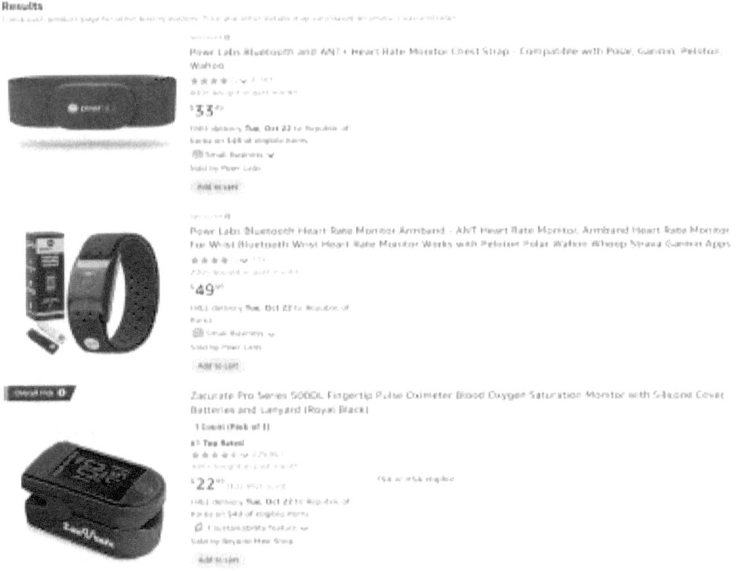

I scrolled through various devices, noting that professional-grade equipment came with hefty price tags. "Well, these must be the kind of machines you'd find in a hospital." As I contemplated selecting items in the $20 to $50 range, it suddenly struck me that my smartphone had an app capable of measuring heart rate.

The day began like any other. Morning sunlight streamed through the window, and I steeled myself to search for evidence of anxiety hidden within my ordinary life. I took out my smartphone and, with a few taps, launched the app. "Measurement start," I commanded.

The first measurement came after I had my coffee. That morning, I treated myself to a shot of my favorite blend from the café. As the strong aroma brushed against my nose, the anxiety began to creep into my mind. The app's screen changed, and the graph shot upwards. "Wow... does it really race this fast?"

"Will I write well today?" The moment that thought crossed my mind, my heart raced even quicker. 100, 110, 120…"Why is it beating so fast? Is it because my livelihood depends on it?"

2024.10.22. / Weather: Overcast

Two days later, I conducted the second experiment. That evening, I found myself waiting for an email from the POD independent publishing site, which would determine whether I had won the high-quality cover design. I sought to measure the anxiety that had built up within me.

Sitting on the sofa, I clutched my smartphone in my hand. The cold metal against my skin pulled me out of the daydream I was ensnared in, grounding me back in reality. The wait for the email morphed into a tangible anxiety, and my heart began to race once again. I tried to cast a spell over my thoughts, whispering to myself, "It's okay if I don't win." Yet, the flicker of unease refused to be extinguished.

I opened the app and started measuring. The numbers on the screen fluctuated rapidly, with my heart rate climbing to 130. "Am I really this sensitive? Who knew a simple decision about a book cover could wield such power over my world?"

Just then, a notification popped up in the bottom right corner of my computer screen. My fingers trembled slightly as I clicked on the   alert.

From: "Bookk" info@bookk.co.kr
To: cyhchs12@naver.com
Cc:
Sent: October 22, 2024 (Thu) 11:03:16 (GMT+09:00)
Subject: [Regarding the Brunch Event] Hello from Bookk

Hello,

This is Bookk.

We are reaching out to inform you that you have been selected for the Brunch Event you applied for on our site!

As a member, you can choose one premium cover design for your publication.

Please select one of the premium cover options available on the Bookk site and let us know via this email. We will ensure that the selected cover is used for your publication.

Please note that premium covers can also be purchased by other users, so if you find a design you like, it's essential to respond as quickly as possible to proceed.

After reviewing this email, we kindly ask you to send us your selection.

Thank you!

'Selection' was the first word that caught my eye. In that moment, the rhythm of my heart surged to its peak. Was this joy? Or, in its truest sense, happiness?

The number before me read 145. Yet, inexplicably, I felt a void amidst this rush of elevated emotion. My body reacted to the long-neglected exhilaration, but could this heartbeat truly signify happiness?

For a while, my heart raced at its highest pitch before gradually descending. Indeed, emotions like joy and happiness felt like strangers in a world I had meticulously constructed. My formula intertwined with the pain waves stemming from my father's death—a complex tapestry of grief. In that emotional landscape, there was no room for uplifting words like happiness or joy. Within the data I had studied, joy was nothing but a distorted emotion, a byproduct of manipulated statistics. "Ah, this wasn't joy…"

Pleasure and happiness flit away like elusive winds—briefly touching, then gone. A gust drifting across the desert may momentarily dampen my skin but fades almost immediately. According to Einstein's theory of relativity, time is not absolute, and perhaps emotions are not either. Joy and sorrow, pleasure and pain are named in reference to their contrasts; thus, the emotions we experience can only be measured against one another.

"Time does not exist. It is but an illusion," Einstein once said.

If that is true, then happiness and joy are likewise transient illusions. The joy felt in this moment will not linger; yet, thanks to that illusion, we can gauge the depths of our pain and sorrow. One cannot exist without the other. It is within our suffering that we come to recognize happiness. Pleasure is merely a fleeting wave of relative emotion, and when that wave subsides, an emptiness remains. In that void, we await another surge of feeling.

Good and evil, destruction and creation, chaos and order, love and hate…

2024.10.26. / Weather: Overcast, then Rain

As the weekend approached, the passage of time felt strangely nebulous. Since leaving my job, the distinction between weekdays and weekends had dissolved, rendering the two days almost meaningless. Yet outside, life pulsed with its usual fervor. The streets, crowded as ever, stirred an inexplicable discomfort within me, a discordant symphony of existence juxtaposed against my quiet solitude.

Late in the afternoon, I found refuge in a café in Dunsan-dong. I ordered a cup of coffee and allowed my gaze to drift across the room. Laughter and animated chatter enveloped me as people relished the long-awaited reprieve from their routines. Yet, as time passed, this vibrant noise morphed into an insidious tide, gnawing at my sense of peace. The mingling of jubilant voices—bragging about wealth, recounting parental triumphs, debating stocks and real estate—intertwined with the persistent whir of the coffee machine, each sound becoming a grain of anxiety lodged in my chest.

I retrieved my smartphone, fingers trembling slightly as I initiated a measurement. 110, 120. The moment my internal unease transformed into cold, hard data, dinner time arrived, prompting a gradual exodus from the café. One by one, patrons abandoned their seats, and as the clamor began to fade, my heart rate surged. 140, 150... "Why is it climbing?"

I drifted beyond the bounds of normalcy, ensnared by the red graph unfurling on the screen. The relentless pounding of my heart resonated in my ears, and even as I attempted to steady my breath, the unease clung to me like a shadow. I cradled the coffee cup, exhaling softly, yet within me, that anxiety had already woven itself into the fabric of my being. "What kind of pain does this anxiety signify?"

As Saturday slipped away, I meticulously organized the data I had gathered over time. There was a peculiar fascination in watching how the intensity of my daily anxieties could be captured and expressed numerically. I realized, with a growing sense of dread, that the weight of my unease continued to press upon me, even in moments I remained blissfully unaware. The numbers lurking within my troubled mind began to murmur: "This is your true pain!"

Data is an unerring witness. The anxiety I encountered daily tightened its grip on me, often unnoticed, yet those moments accumulated, guiding my very existence. Now, these figures representing my anxiety had transcended mere numbers; they embodied the essence of my true suffering.

The Tools of Sorrow

After gathering data on my anxiety, I resolved to keep an emotional journal. This wasn't just about quantifying the depths of my feelings; I wanted to understand how these emotions impacted my life.

A week ago, I wrote "Diary of Sorrow" at the top of the first page of an A4 sheet. Each day, I reflected on my emotional state. When I woke up in the morning, the overcast sky outside deepened my sadness. "What will the end of today feel like?"

This A4 sheet became a small vessel to contain the weight of my heart. I decided to rate my emotions on a scale from 1 to 10, where 1 meant "no feelings at all" and 10 indicated "unbearable pain." On the first day, I rated my sorrow a 6. "It's not that serious yet."

On the second day, sadness continued to press heavily on my heart. That day, I met up with a high school friend. Despite the joy of reconnecting, our conversation was laden with a profound sadness. To preserve that moment, I described the scene in detail. "During our conversation, he brought up the topic of his father. In that instant, a pang shot through my chest, and my sorrow deepened. My emotional score rose to 8." By documenting these emotions, I was able to anticipate how the numbers might change. Through specific episodes, I quantitatively measured the depth of my sorrow.

Just as I had done with my anxiety data, after a week of recording, I organized the sorrow scores and created a neat little table.

The Tools of Anger

I utilized a household massager that had been lying around in the living room. This device is designed to relieve muscle tension, so I thought it could help measure changes in my anger.

On the first day, before using the massager, I asked myself what triggers my anger. Gripping the massager, I recalled the discomfort I felt during a conversation with my family while preparing dinner.

The refrigerator didn't contain anything particularly special, but I found some leftover vegetables and a few pieces of tofu. I chopped onions, minced garlic, and added oil to the heated pan, sautéing the vegetables in order. The fluffy rice hit the pan with a cheerful sound.

As I was finishing dinner preparations, my mother approached the table. With a hint of sarcasm, she asked, "How have you been doing these days?"

"Just fine, you know."

"Are you a writer yet? When will you get a real job? They say SRT isn't bad either."

My mother always had this way about her. Each time she reached out to talk, it felt like she was holding a sweet candy in one hand and a sharp little needle in the other.

Her tone was encouraging, but it didn't take long to grasp the underlying message. It had always been like that. My mother would say, "I'll support you no matter what you do!" only to follow it up with, "But you can write even when you're in your 40s or 50s. Why don't you just find a stable job for now?"

Support mingled with shadows of doubt. As a child, I accepted her words as mere advice, but as an adult, I realized they had led me into confusion.

Even when I achieved something, she would present another standard, implying that it wasn't enough. The moment I recognized this pattern in our conversations, her words often pierced my heart like arrows, lodging themselves deep within. Such contradictory messages were sufficient to evoke a sense of emptiness.

Note: In the context of this work, "SRT" refers to a rapid transit system in South Korea that is a popular choice for commuters. It stands for "Super Rapid Train," which is an efficient mode of transportation. Providing this clarification helps non-Korean readers understand its relevance in the narrative.

I tried to calm my breathing by rolling a grain of rice on the dining table. Yet, my mother's words, "You can always write later," ignited a slow burn of anger within me. It was as if I had doused a fading ember with oil. Chewing on the fried rice in my mouth, I mulled over that uncomfortable question.

A conversation that fails to make anything whole. The subtle incompleteness of it weighed down on me, and soon enough, anger rose steadily to the top of my head. I thought there could be no more discomforting feeling than realizing that those I called family felt so estranged.

As the fried rice in the pan dwindled to nothing, the air around the table thickened with tension. After carelessly stacking the dishes in the sink, I retreated to my room and pressed the power button on the massager. I wanted to shake off those uncomfortable emotions, even if just for a moment. As I relaxed my legs, thoughts of that earlier conversation lingered. The stronger the massager's vibrations grew, the more I felt I could visualize my anger.

On the second day, I resolved to summon memories of the past and observe my emotions with greater precision. Beneath the large bookshelf next to my writing desk, in a narrow space barely 60 centimeters wide, there lay a delivery box. Before reaching for it, I glanced at the box curled up in that corner. It had been buried there for seven long months, hidden behind thick books and the heavy shadows of knowledge, gathering dust. Its surface had faded with time, and tiny specks of dust accumulated along its edges, mirroring the silence of that space, void of any breeze, which felt just like a corner of my heart.

Inside was a Chanel WOC handbag I had sent to my ex-girlfriend—a parting gift she had returned to me the moment she received it.

As I pulled the box out, a strange feeling washed over me. 'No matter how hard I try, my feelings just don't get through.' Regret and longing intersected, and I decided to imbue meaning into that box.

Carefully peeling the tape with a cutter knife, I revealed the beautifully wrapped Chanel WOC. Once a symbol of love, this object now embodied my failure and helplessness. Without sincerity, this bag would merely be a hollow mound of money. "Material things... cannot rule the human spirit."

The pent-up anger slowly raised its head. Was my sincerity, my heart, destined to return in such a manner? I could no longer contain the emotions bubbling inside as I stared at the box. Without hesitation, I grabbed the massager, placing it on my lap, and turned up the intensity of its vibrations. With each rhythmic pulse stimulating my skin, the sharp little anger began to spread throughout my body. The vibrations flowed down my legs, making me feel as though my emotions were being quantified physically.

"Right now, the intensity of anger has reached 7.5," I muttered to myself, watching the waves of my anger rise and fall as they coursed through me. After stopping the massager, I began to jot down my thoughts in my notebook.

"The returned delivery box containing the Chanel WOC ultimately reflected the feelings I had failed to communicate. Through vibrations, my anger transformed into a tangible emotion, and I could feel its weight more clearly."

A week later, I analyzed the patterns of my anger. I identified specific situations that triggered it, such as heated moments during family conversations or when uncontrollable rage flared up. For instance, during those moments, I would increase the massager's pressure or allocate more time to its use. When my anger peaked, I applied stronger pressure with the device, gradually reducing it over time. Through this process, I realized I could manage my anger.

Lastly, based on the recorded data, I organized the pressure intensity according to each incident: "A pressure of 5 for the rude café staff, 7 for the conflict in my mother's mixed messages, and 9 for the emotions surrounding my ex-girlfriend's feelings." I compiled this in Excel and visualized the patterns of my anger through graphs. This exercise was not just about recording anger; it became a way to analyze the amplitude of the emotions I experienced. I engraved in my mind that anger does not control me; rather, it is a path to understanding myself better.

Final Verification

My personal formula for emotions seemed to fit perfectly. Yet, a sense of emptiness began to creep in from a corner of my mind. Despite the neatly completed equations in my head, something felt off, lacking tangible substance.

"What's missing?"

After finishing my workout at the gym, I stepped into the shower. To cool my overheated body, I turned on the cold water, but the initial touch of the water felt as frigid as ice. A shiver coursed through my entire body, so intense that I could hardly catch my breath. Yet, after a few seconds, my frozen body started to acclimate, and the icy water gradually felt more comfortable.

"Oh right. If pain can dull over time, can emotions also adapt so easily?"As I finished showering and stepped out, I accidentally bumped into the wall. A sharp pain shot through my arm and into my head. This time, however, the pain didn't subside as quickly as the cold water had. It lingered. Even after five minutes, my heart raced, and the pain continued to torment me.

Pain was different from other sensations. It didn't easily diminish with time; its intensity didn't immediately fade. This pain, I realized, couldn't be adapted to, and that was the essence of "threshold."

"If there's no threshold for pain, that moment could pose a significant risk to life. Does the pain I felt in my relationship with my father become sharper, more vivid, as time goes on?"

My formula needed a threshold. Between sensation and pain lies a moment that transcends intensity. Without calculating the threshold of pain, this equation would simply be a sequence of numbers.

Pain imprints itself more sharply and powerfully at the moment it surpasses the threshold. The reason we don't acquiesce to pain is that it serves as a vital warning signal for survival. To calculate that threshold, I needed a formula capable of unraveling how sensations morph into pain. Just as bright light can sting the eyes, loud sounds can hurt the ears, and pressure beyond a certain point can lead to pain, I needed to express these boundaries mathematically.

2024.10.30. / Weather: Overcast

The transformation of visual stimuli into pain occurs when the intensity of light entering the eye—known as illuminance—exceeds a certain threshold. Excessive light can damage the optic nerve, leading to pain. The threshold for visual stimuli is denoted as light intensity L, and the light stimuli that exceed this threshold are defined as follows:

Visual Pain Equation:

$$\mathrm{Pain_{vision}} = \alpha_1(L - L_{\mathrm{threshold}})$$

- L: Light intensity (lumens)

- $L_{\mathrm{threshold}}$: Threshold of light at which pain is perceived

- α_1: Coefficient determining the sensitivity of visual pain

Experimental Tools:Lux measurement app on my smartphone

On a weekend morning, I sat by the window, gazing at the blinding sun. I opened the lux measurement app installed on my smartphone and pointed the screen toward the sunlight. As the reading climbed and surpassed 800 lux, a gradual pain began to wash over my eyes. The discomfort intensified quietly, overwhelming all my visual senses. While recording this, I wondered, "Can the pain associated with the threshold be quantified?"

I reached out with one hand toward the dazzling sun, while my other hand recorded the changing numbers on the app in real time. Squinting slightly, I noted, "500 lux: slight stimulation, no pain."

The longer I stared at the sun, the more intense the light became. The number on the screen crossed 600, moving toward 700. It felt as if a mirage was rising before my eyes, and the signals of pain began to gradually stimulate my nerves. I placed my finger back on the smartphone and recorded again. "700 lux: mild pain, eye fatigue."

Once it exceeded 800 lux, it felt as though I had thrown my eyes into a blazing furnace. The optic nerve was overloaded, and a peculiar discomfort settled within my eyes. I could hear a popping sound in my brain. I continued to record. "800 lux: pain in the eyes, blurred vision."

Even rubbing my eyes didn't easily alleviate the pain. When I checked the smartphone screen again, it read 850. A strong ache radiated from my forehead and temples. I took a deep breath and noted, "850 lux: intensified pain, strong pressure in the forehead and temples."

"870..." The numbers kept climbing. "How much light-induced pain can I endure?"I thought as I struggled to keep my eyes on the smartphone. "900 lux: intense pain, eyelids involuntarily closing, severe headache."

I turned away from the window. My vision momentarily darkened, and I could see nothing. "At what point do the optic nerves transition from discomfort to pain? 800 lux, 850 lux..."

I reviewed the data recorded in the app. The precise moment when light intensity transitions into pain—that was the answer I sought: the threshold of vision. I could clearly distinguish the onset and peak of the pain. "Pain begins at 800 lux and reaches its maximum at 850 lux."

This time, I covered my eyes with both hands and faced the light once more. This time, I focused not on the numerical value of illuminance, but on the flow of pain created within me by that light. "This pain striking my optic nerves—does the pain of my emotions rise within me in the same way?"

2024.11.01. / Weather: Clear

Auditory stimuli can trigger pain when the volume and frequency of sounds increase. Especially, when the vibrations become too intense, the eardrum can no longer withstand it, and tinnitus may occur. Sound intensity is measured in decibels (dB), and stimuli that exceed the threshold can be described as follows:

Auditory Pain Equation:

$$\text{Pain}_{\text{auditory}} = \alpha_2(S - S_{\text{threshold}})$$

- S: Sound intensity (decibels)

- $S_{\text{threshold}}$: Threshold of sound at which pain is perceived

- α_2: Coefficient determining the sensitivity of auditory pain

EXPERIMENTAL TOOL: Sound measurement app on a smartphone.

I was meeting an old high school friend for the first time in a while, having fried chicken and beer for dinner. We caught up on each other's lives, reminiscing about our high school homeroom teacher. Suddenly, the sound of a glass breaking came from one side of the restaurant, followed by the clattering of metal utensils and pans from the kitchen, interspersed with laughter mixed with shouting. I opened the sound measurement app on my phone and began measuring the surrounding noise levels. My friend kept asking me what I was doing, but I gestured for him to be quiet, signaling with my hand as I needed to focus on the other sounds.

At 80 dB, I felt my eardrums start to pulse slowly with an unpleasant twinge of pain. "What kind of pain could this noise be inflicting on me?"

The restaurant grew louder as more people, now drunk, began standing up and shouting toasts at the neighboring table. Each time their chairs scraped the floor, a sharp noise followed. "75 dB..." The number scrolled across the screen nonchalantly. Then the restaurant door burst open with a group of four college students shouting, "Second round's on us! Chicken and beer!" The noise was so loud my ears buzzed. I glanced at the screen again: the number hit 80 dB.

I opened a new file, labeling it The Moment When Sound Transforms Into Pain, and I began recording every moment in detail. 75 dB: pressure on the eardrum. Discomfort. Mild pain. Every time the laughter from the next table grew louder, my eardrums picked up on the subtle stimulation. It felt like a light prick with a needle, but it was a familiar level of noise for a pub. 80 dB: occasional thuds in the eardrum. Slight pain.

Suddenly, someone cursed loudly and slammed their beer glass onto the floor. "Crash! Hey! What the hell? Why are you starting shit?" Three bulky men, seemingly fueled by alcohol and perhaps the presence of a woman nearby, grabbed each other by the collars and hurled a string of obscenities.

My friend suggested we pay and leave, but I couldn't let this golden opportunity slip by. As the shouting and cursing escalated, the sound struck my eardrums like a hammer, surpassing mere discomfort and becoming real pain. That was the turning point—the moment when pain truly set in. 85 dB: sound penetrates the brain. Anxiety ensues. Pain intensifies.

As the noise level climbed, the pain that started in my eardrums surged toward my brain. The higher the decibels climbed, the more indescribable the pain became. "This pain doesn't originate solely from the nerves. As the numbers increase, the pain connects to the brain and merges with my psychological anxiety."

I ignored the escalating brawl, my friend's insistence that we move to a quieter bar, and focused solely on the numbers displayed on my screen. I had to explore how these figures connected with my emotions.

90 dB: unbearable level. Peak of pain. Explosion of emotions linked to nerves. My friend finally walked out.

The restaurant owner intervened to break up the fight, but my eardrums couldn't bear it any longer. Even with my eyes closed, the shouting reverberated in my head. At that moment, I realized that the threshold of painwasn't just a neurological reaction but an emotional one intertwined with nerve stimulation.

"Could such wretched noise be connected to inner emotional pain?" As the decibels rose, the noise began to touch the shallow layers of my emotions, deepening into a more profound pain.

I went to the counter to pay, only to be told by the cashier that my friend had already covered it. Outside, my friend gestured repeatedly, covering his ears, urging me to hurry up and follow him outside.

A police car was approaching the restaurant as we finally stepped outside and began walking slowly down the street, away from the chaos.

The evening breeze was pleasantly cool. He suggested a walk, saying he was full, and I nodded quietly. Walking helped cool my mind, still rattled from the noise. As we strolled, a perfume shop caught my eye with its particularly elaborate display.

"Shall we step in for a moment?" I thought smelling various scents might help stimulate different senses, which could assist with my research on pain. I nodded again, and we stepped into the shop together.

Olfactory Stimuli: When the concentration of certain chemicals becomes too high, it irritates the nerves, leading to pain. Particularly pungent odors can stimulate both the nose and brain's cortex, causing intense discomfort and pain. Imagine the stench of an old-fashioned outhouse in a rural area to understand how severe this can be. The threshold for olfactory stimulation is determined by the chemical concentration, C.

Olfactory Pain Equation:

$$\text{Pain}_{\text{olfactory}} = \alpha_5(O - O_{\text{threshold}})$$

- O: Odor intensity (concentration of odorant)
- $O_{\text{threshold}}$: Threshold of odor at which pain is perceived
- α_5: Coefficient determining the sensitivity of olfactory pain

Experiment Tool: Perfumes and food.

As soon as we stepped inside, a multitude of fragrances enveloped me. If only the scent belonged to a woman... but instead, it was a blend of sweet vanilla, warm musk, sharp citrus, and heavy wood. "Baseline: Multiple mixed scents in the air. No particular discomfort."

An employee approached and said, "Feel free to try it on your wrist." I carefully chose a citrus-based perfume. "I'll sample this one."

As soon as I sprayed it on my wrist, a sharp fragrance hit my nose. The tangy scent of lemon mixed with the sharpness of grapefruit, pricking at my nostrils. "Initial stimulus: Citrus scent pricks the nose. No discomfort. No pain. Not a bad scent."

Once the employee moved on to another customer, I sprayed the perfume twice more on my wrist. As the scent deepened, the stimulation grew stronger. My nose tingled, and I felt the chemicals slowly coursing through my brain. "Second stimulus: Citrus scent intensifies, causing a prickling sensation. Pain score: 3/10."

I continued inhaling the scent directly from my wrist. My head began to feel light, and tears welled slightly in the corners of my eyes. "Third stimulus: Allergic reaction. Pain spreads from nose to head. Pain score: 6/10."

I stretched my arm out and inhaled again from a distance, but the sharp citrus still stung my nose and throbbed in my head. Whether it was an allergic reaction or pure pain, the discomfort gradually morphed into real agony. "Ugh, I'm getting dizzy," I muttered under my breath.

My friend, now finished picking a perfume for his girlfriend, came over and said, "What have you been doing this whole time? Let's go, I already bought mine." As we stepped out, I sprayed the perfume three more times on my wrist. 'Chik, chik, chik,' and as I brought my wrist to my nose again on our way out, "Final stimulus: Peak of pain. Irritation lingers in nasal passages and deep within the head. Pain score: 8/10." "Conclusion: Citrus scent induces deep nasal and head irritation, causing a pain score of approximately 7-8. Olfactory threshold starts around 3 and rises to 8."

We stepped out of the bustling city streets and headed toward a Korean restaurant. Earlier, my friend had mentioned that he couldn't eat much of the chicken because it was too noisy, and now he suggested grabbing some late-night food. As I thought about it, I realized that taste, too, could be linked to pain. Spiciness, excessive sweetness, or bitterness can cross the threshold from taste to pain. The intensity of taste stimuli is measured by the concentration of specific chemical substances, and when that concentration surpasses a certain threshold, the taste stimulus transforms into pain.

Gustatory Pain Equation:

$$\text{Pain}_{\text{gustatory}} = \alpha_4(G - G_{\text{threshold}})$$

- G: Taste intensity (scale of sweetness/sourness)

- $G_{\text{threshold}}$: Threshold of taste at which pain is perceived

- α_4: Coefficient determining the sensitivity of gustatory pain

EXPERIMENTAL TOOL: Spicy food

I ordered the spiciest braised short ribs on the menu. The dish was packed with Cheongyang peppers, radiating a fierce red color that was almost overwhelming just by sight. I was curious to see at what point my sense of taste would hit its limit. This restaurant was known for attracting people who wanted to challenge their tolerance for spicy food, and they achieved this level of heat without using capsaicin extracts. As someone who enjoys spicy food, I saw this as a worthy challenge, and my mouth was watering in anticipation. My friend, on the other hand, only stared at my ribs with longing, as he couldn't handle spicy food and had ordered a mild puffer fish soup instead.

But my goal wasn't just to enjoy the spiciness of the short ribs. I was sitting there to record the exact moment when the spicy sensation would cross the threshold into pain. Before picking up my spoon, I opened the notepad on my phone to record my baseline. "Baseline: No spicy stimuli. Tongue and mouth are in a normal state."

The smell of the peppers began to tease my nose, and soon my tongue started reacting to the intense aroma. The steam rose from the dish, and the broth was bubbling in a fiery red pool filled with peppers and seasonings. I took my first spoonful. The sharp tingle on the tip of my tongue slowly spread to the roof of my mouth and down my throat. I immediately noted it in my phone: "First stimulus: A tingling sensation on the tip of the tongue. Pain index: 2/10. Mere stimulation, no pain."

The more I ate, the stronger the spiciness became. By the time the second spoonful slid down my throat, the pain became more distinct. My tongue began to burn, my entire mouth felt hot, my heart started racing slightly, and beads of sweat formed around my eyes and forehead. "Second stimulus: Tongue and throat burning. Pain index: 5/ 10. Spiciness gradually shifting into pain."

As expected, the intense heat of the peppers didn't take long to overwhelm my senses. The spiciness spread throughout my mouth, and my tongue, palate, and throat all felt like they were on fire. Every sense in my body felt like it was becoming numb. Even breathing was painful. My lips burned the most, like they were engulfed in flames. I tried to cool the pain by gulping down cold water, but it only provided temporary relief. The pain refused to subside. "Third stimulus: Pain reaching its peak. Pain index: 7/10. Spicy stimuli transmitted to the brain, accompanied by a headache."

The experiment wasn't over yet. I took the last bite of the short ribs, spooning it into my mouth. "Fourth stimulus: Pain at its zenith. Pain index: 9/10. Taste buds numbed. Physical reactions include sweating, tearing, and increased heart rate."

"Conclusion: Spiciness turns into pain at a level of 7/10, and at 9/10, it leads to nerve numbness and physical responses. The threshold for taste begins at approximately 6 and peaks at 9."

"I've surpassed what I can handle. This is the threshold."

I put down my spoon and documented the moment when the spicy sensation morphed into pain. Pain wasn't something imposed from the outside. I realized how it depended on how my body processed it, how my nerves converted that intense stimulus into pain.

"Are you done? You look like you're about to die. Should I get you a yogurt drink?"

"You, with your bland soup—come try this. It's amazing."

"Yeah, no. I can't handle spice. No way."

After paying for the meal, we stepped outside, my friend grinning, clearly pleased after both chicken and late-night food. We walked for another ten minutes before parting ways since we were heading in different directions. Even as I made my way home, the spicy burn occasionally resurfaced, making me feel a little nauseous. After wrapping up the evening with an old high school friend, I lay down on my bed without even bothering to shower.

→ **Today's takeaway: Thresholds for pain calculated for three senses (hearing, smell, taste).**

2024.11.06. / Weather: Cloudy after rain

Touch can easily transform into pain through pressure or temperature changes. Especially, extreme pressure or sudden temperature shifts stimulate nerve endings in the skin, triggering pain. The intensity of these stimuli is represented by pressure PP Pand temperature T T T , and by comparing them to their thresholds, one can calculate the magnitude of pain.

Tactile Pain Sensitivity Expression:

The tactile pain sensitivity can be expressed with the following parameters:

- α_s: Sensitivity constant for tactile stimuli, encompassing both pressure and temperature effects.

- **P_threshold**: Threshold value for pressure.

- **T_threshold**: Threshold value for temperature.

- T: Intensity of temperature (in degrees Celsius).

The relationship can be summarized in the following formula:

$$\text{Pain}_{\text{tactile}} = \alpha_s \cdot ((P - P_{\text{threshold}}) + (T - T_{\text{threshold}}))$$

Where:

- P: Pressure applied (in Pascals).

EXPERIMENT TOOLS: ICE Pack

Today felt especially heavy. Writing requires a touch of creativity, and with stress building up, my body had stiffened as if turned to stone. On days like this, I head to the gym without fail. Exercise helped me release the tension that accumulated, easing the fatigue left in my muscles. The gym was just five minutes from my house, and as usual, heavy dumbbells and weight machines awaited me. I started with deadlifts, an exercise that engages the core muscles, utilizing strength from the hips, back, and legs. Slowly, I placed my hands on the dumbbell, feeling its weight before lifting it all at once. As the load rose from the floor, my body bore the brunt of the immense pressure.

After finishing the first set, I felt a dull ache in my back. It wasn't pain, more like a natural pressure from the strain. I wondered how this sensation might evolve into actual pain. For the second set, I increased the weight—100kg, then 110kg, and finally 120kg. The moment the weight increased, the pressure on my back, legs, and wrists shifted noticeably. Each time I lifted, my palms clenched the dumbbell harder, leaving marks on the skin. The imprint of the weight turned my skin red as the pressure intensified, transmitting that sensation to my brain.

By the time the final set ended, my back was stiff, and my legs felt like heavy anchors dragging my body downward. It was time to experiment with the threshold of pressure. "How much more pressure can I endure?"I spread out a mat and lay down, lowering my hips and back onto the floor. Then, I moved to the leg press machine, engaging the muscles in my legs. As the footplate descended, it felt like an enormous weight was crashing down onto my legs. The load reached 150kg, and I absorbed it through my soles and thighs. My legs began to tremble as the weight bore down on my muscles, and I reached the point where the fatigue crossed over into pain. "This must be the pain threshold."

When the final set was over, I collapsed onto the floor, gasping for breath as I reflected on the weight of the pressure. Now, the pressure I felt wasn't just a physical sensation; it had fully transformed into pain. Without my trainer's help, I knew my body couldn't take much more. After finishing my workout and returning home, my body sank into a heavy state of exhaustion. My back and hips were tense, and the pain spread like a slow, dull ache. I knew I had to find some way to relieve the accumulated tension, so I quickly grabbed an ice pack from the freezer. I wondered how much relief this small pack of ice could provide.

"Baseline: Pain level 7/10 in the back and hips. Muscles feel tight, with a dull, persistent ache."

I gently placed the ice pack on my lower back and hips. "Ah, that's cold."The cold sensation traveled across the surface of my skin, and it felt as though my body was freezing over. The cold began to soothe the pain little by little. "First stimulus: Cold sensation spreads across the skin. Pain level: 6/10. Slight relief."

As the cold penetrated deeper into the muscles, the pain slowly dissipated. The stiffness in my back began to ease, and the pain subsided more rapidly. Now, the pain was turning into a sense of relief. "Second stimulus: Cold seeps deeper into the muscles, reducing pain. Pain level: 4/10. Muscles relaxing."

After a few more minutes, the cold sensation began to stimulate my nerves more than the pain did. The pain, now down to a 4, continued to drop, and soon the cold sensation completely replaced it. "Third stimulus: Pain almost gone. Pain level: 2/10. Nerves calming. Cold replaces pain."

I made note of everything. I pressed the ice pack harder onto my back, letting the cold permeate even further. That cold had penetrated deep into my body.

"Final stimulus: Pain gone. Pain level: 0/10. The ice pack has fully covered the pain. Only the cold sensation remains."

2024.11.30. / Weather: Overcast

Now, by integrating the five distinct stimuli, we can formulate a comprehensive equation that represents the total sum of pain. Essentially, I could now unify the process where sensations cross their thresholds and transform into pain into a single formula.

★ Composite Pain Equation

Total Pain Equation:

$$\text{Total Pain} = \sum_{i=1}^{5} \alpha_i \cdot (S_i - S_{i,\text{threshold}})$$

- S_i: Sensory intensity (vision, hearing, touch, taste, smell)

- $S_{i,\text{threshold}}$: Threshold of sensory intensity for each sense

- α_i: Coefficient determining the sensitivity of each sensory pain

$\cdot$ SI= PAIN(X) = AC^2 + βP^3 + γD

Morning sunlight gently brushed past the window. I sat with a cup of coffee before me, sinking into a quiet sea of thought. "Let's start here," I muttered to myself. "If I strip away the complexity of the equation and create a simplified model, I might be able to apply it to everyday life." A pencil was in my hand, and I began pouring simple formulas onto the paper.

Anxiety, sorrow, anger—these three emotions are all intertwined.

Pain = (1 × Anxiety) + (2 × Sorrow) + (3 × Anger): A Simplified Model of Real-Life Experiences

When compared to the composite equation, this simplified model felt as unstable as a sandcastle built on the rough surface of an old abacus. Still, the composite equation was too cumbersome to capture the finer grains of everyday pain. The small frustrations, the stress of daily life, the irritations from conversations, the regret over minor mistakes—these didn't all need to be absorbed into some grand equation. What I needed was something more intuitive.

Anxiety was assigned a light value of 1. Yet, that very lightness made it the most frequent element of pain in daily life. Sorrow, with a value of 2, deepened the weight of suffering. Anger, carrying the largest value of 3, symbolized the explosive escalation of pain.

The reason I chose to simplify pain in this way was to better understand and manage my emotions right now—before I had to face the overwhelming reality of my father's death. I had to dissect the smaller daily pains first.

Yet, part of me questioned, "Can such a complex thing as emotion really be reduced to simple numbers?"But as someone who barely understood my own emotions—let alone the emotions of others—I had no choice but to bridge the gap between numbers and feelings like this.

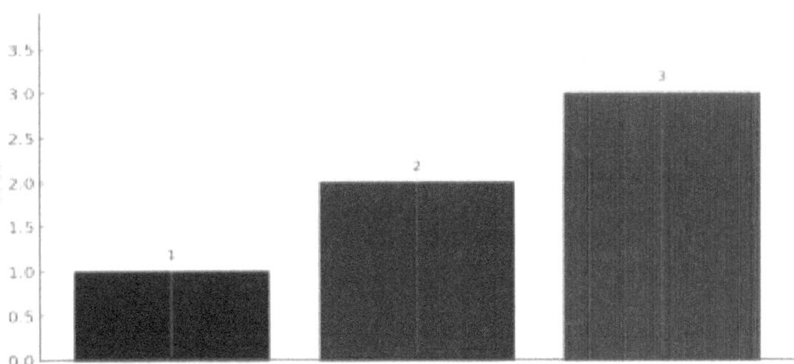

AS I LAID OUT THE COMPOSITE equation and the simplified model before me, I felt as if the weight of my emotions lightened ever so slightly. "A measure of pain—it's fascinating, but also somewhat futile."

Time had slipped by like a gentle wave. Outside, the leaves rustled in the wind, and the morning sunlight wrapped my room in its warm embrace while I remained absorbed in my inner experiment.

Three weeks ago, when the mysterious email arrived, I hadn't known what to feel. But day by day, as I accumulated more data, I started to observe my emotions with a more serious, focused gaze. I quantified my morning anxiety as I tasted the bitterness of my coffee. I pinched my arm to gauge the intensity of my anger. And I measured the depth of my sorrow by recording the ache that throbbed in my back.

My research often took place in the shadow of unbearable pain. And while I crafted these equations, that email would drift back into my mind, unsettling me. At first, I wondered, "Should I reply?" But the fear of stirring up old wounds held my fingers frozen. I couldn't bring myself to move even an inch.

Many times, I sat at the computer, trying to write a response, but my hands refused to touch the keys. In the end, I let the email slide by. At this point, when I lacked the courage to answer, that email only served to amplify my anxiety and dread. Like the irretrievable past with my father, the email seemed to demand a response from me—a decision I was too afraid to make.

Each time I opened my inbox, its title stared back at me, unrelenting. Even that felt like a trigger, a constant reminder of the pain I was trying to ignore. It became not just a stimulant for my distress but a convenient excuse to avoid confronting it.

(The blue box above : [Brunch Story] A New Proposal Has Arrived for You! - This is an email related to a question concerning the father.)

Q. IF I WERE TO BREAK down the mysterious email using the Composite Pain Equation, what would the value be?

A. ?

Total Pain Equation:

$$\text{Total Pain} = \sum_{i=1}^{5} \alpha_i \cdot (S_i - S_{i,\text{threshold}})$$

- S_i: Sensory intensity (vision, hearing, touch, taste, smell)

- $S_{i,\text{threshold}}$: Threshold of sensory intensity for each sense

- α_i: Coefficient determining the sensitivity of each sensory pain

● PAIN VALUE AND THRESHOLD / Set Pain Threshold / Intensity· Anxiety (S1):Pain value 3 / (S1, threshold): 1 / α1: 1
  · Sorrow (S2):Pain value 4 / (S2, threshold): 2 / α2: 2
  · Anger (S3):Pain value 2 / (S3, threshold): 1 / α3: 1
  · Anxiety: $1 \times (3 - 1) = 2$
  · Sorrow: $2 \times (4 - 2) = 4$
  · Anger: $1 \times (2 - 1) = 1$
  ∴ Total Pain $= 2 + 4 + 1 = 7$

At the moment I received the email, my pain index was 7. As the sky began to fade and the lights quietly receded, I curled up in the corner of my room, replaying the contents of the email over and over again in my mind. The value of 7 felt like a subtle tightening of my chest, each breath a little harder than the last. That number—it represented more than just a moment of pain. It was a reflection of my father's fate, a fate I knew I would face someday.

Could the number 7, then, also be tied to the secret hidden in his coat? I checked the numbers again and laid back down in bed, staring at the ceiling, trying to piece it all together.

Chapter 3: Loneliness

DECEMBER 1, 2024./ Weather: First Snow

I don't understand why my hair grows so fast. Staring into the mirror, I looked at the rough, sharp ends poking out. The sideburns stretching down to my chin were especially unsightly. But what connection could there possibly be between overgrown hair and loneliness? Loneliness, like my hair, seemed to quietly and slowly envelop me.

It was an early winter afternoon, rain pouring down as I headed to the barbershop. Just as I turned the corner of the building, I noticed a drenched cat huddling miserably against the rain. Its pale gray fur hung limply as it sheltered beneath the canopy of a window outside a one-room apartment. The cat and I locked eyes, and we stood there, both staring blankly at each other.

'Have I lived my life like that cat? A voluntary outsider?' I'd avoided socializing with others, always choosing solitude.

Yes,I thought, I've been like a cat.Cold, independent, and never leaning on anyone.

I had always been alone. Friends from high school and college had long stopped calling, and the women I once loved had all left me. If human beings are said to have free will, I could convince myself that my isolation was a choice. But loneliness—that creeps up on you regardless of your will.

Perhaps my father felt the same. He must have been a lonely man. I recalled his face, one that rarely showed emotion.

Will my father's death bring me another wave of loneliness?

Loneliness and solitude are undoubtedly different. Longing stirs waves in your heart as you think of someone or something that has disappeared. But solitude—it comes from the very core of your being. I passed another block, but the image of that cat kept coming back to me. It occurred to me that perhaps the loneliness I felt wasn't just due to broken connections with others or past heartbreaks. It could be, like the cat's nature or inherited traits, that loneliness was something passed down to me from my parents.

A few days later, I came across an ad for puppy adoption by chance. Is there any way to measure loneliness? The thought intrigued me, and I was willing to experiment with this feeling any way I could to find an answer.

I had always wanted a golden retriever, so I made sure to carefully consider all the options. Golden retrievers are known for their loyalty and gentle nature—just what I needed to soothe my loneliness.

Ding-dong

"Hello, you're here to see the puppies, right?" The owner greeted me with a bright smile.

"Yes, hello."

There was something about their small frames, shiny eyes, and that pure, baby-like innocence that made me feel as though they could fill a part of the emptiness inside me. As I stepped into the house, warm sunlight filled the room. Several puppies were there, and one of them slowly made its way toward me. It tilted its head, looking up at me with curious eyes. This one,I thought, this one will do.

After going through some formalities and signing the papers, I felt as though this puppy and I were now bound by fate. What should I name him? Loneliness...

I settled on a name that echoed the feeling of solitude: Solitude.Sol,for short.

The autumn scenery streaming past the window seemed to deepen the feeling of loneliness, but the small life sitting next to me began to lighten the weight of that feeling. Sol climbed into my lap from the passenger seat and curled up quietly, and I could feel his warmth.

That night, as I brought the puppy home, I wondered how to weigh the weight of loneliness. Incidentally, this little one was male, just like my father and me. Once we arrived, he played around for a while before falling into a deep sleep on the cushion under the sofa. Suddenly, I found myself wondering: What role do male animals play as fathers? Using my foot, I picked up the remote and flipped to National Geographic.

Among animals, the concept of "father" was vague. Only a few species had family structures where the male's role resembled that of a human father. Lions and wolves, for example—strong males protected the family and trained their offspring when necessary. But for most other animals, the father's role was purely biological. It was the mother who raised the offspring after the father's departure.

Hmmm...In human society, the father is established as the protector and the pillar of the household. Yet at the same time, he is often the most distant and unfamiliar figure. Fathers, spending most of their time outside, chasing the currency that runs the world, often become alienated from their families. My father had been no exception.

I concluded that "loneliness" as an emotion could not be included in the collection of pain. Loneliness wasn't something that could simply be categorized as a wound or discomfort. After watching TV for about two more hours, I rose from the plush sofa, and suddenly, that peculiar coat came back to mind—the worn coat my father used to wear every time he left for work.

That coat seemed to symbolize my father's loneliness. He never expressed his emotions, so I could never fully grasp what his loneliness truly was. As I alternated between thoughts of his coat and the dog I had brought home, my mind wandered into the past.

The coat might have shielded him, but that cold fabric could never have filled the void of his loneliness. If that were true, then this dog might serve a similar purpose for me. The dog, ever loyal, follows me, but it, too, cannot replace the deep-seated loneliness inside. Could loneliness be expressed in a formula?

The intensity of loneliness starts with absence. My father's parched emotions always approached me like that cold coat, and I had no choice but to swim through the vast emptiness it left behind. While spending time with the dog, I started to adjust the variables of this loneliness. Could the warmth of the dog's presence reduce the variable of loneliness?

Not only the intensity of loneliness but also how it amplifies in certain situations had to be considered. When I touched my father's coat, the stillness did not merely end with sadness. The coldness had absorbed the emptiness brought by his absence. Though the presence of the dog lessened that void, the moment I recalled the coat, the hollowness expanded tenfold.

I decided to use multiplication rather than addition in the equation for loneliness. The intensity of loneliness and the absence of my father didn't just add up—they interacted dynamically, amplifying or diminishing each other, sometimes swelling exponentially, sometimes receding into a mere whisper.

- **$L\_total = A \times L / A$ (Father's Absence), L (Intensity of Loneliness)**

Loneliness Intensity (L):The sheer strength of the emotion itself, a measurement of how strongly I felt loneliness in particular moments.

For example:The intensity of loneliness when I thought of my father's absence or when I was alone.

Absence Impact (A):The magnitude of how my father's absence affected my daily life. This value encompassed not just loneliness but the broader psychological impact of his absence.For example:How much I missed or longed for him, or how his absence caused me pain.

A (Absence Impact):The psychological impact of my father's absence, quantified on a scale from -10 to +10, representing whether his absence affected me positively (e.g., less loneliness, not thinking of him) or negatively (e.g., intensified loneliness).

L (Loneliness Intensity):The intensity of loneliness at a given moment, measured on a scale from 0 to 10, indicating how deeply loneliness permeated in particular instances.

Day 1: Walking the dog

A (Absence Impact): +3 (The dog's company reduced my loneliness)

L (Loneliness Intensity): 5 (Though I briefly thought of my father's absence, the loneliness was not overwhelming)

→ L_total = 3 × 5 = 15

Day 2: My father's coat

A (Absence Impact): -6 (The coat heightened the sense of absence)

L (Loneliness Intensity): 7 (Touching the coat deepened the feeling of loneliness)

→ L_total = -6 × 7 = -42

Day 3: Playing fetch with the dog

A (Absence Impact): +2 (Playing with the dog made me forget the loneliness for a while)

L (Loneliness Intensity): 4 (The game allowed me to momentarily forget the loneliness)

→ L_total = 2 × 4 = 8

I sat down at my desk, staring at a blank sheet of paper. I considered replying to the email, but he and I still couldn't understand each other's emotions. The feelings left unspoken, the awkwardness wedged between us, couldn't be unraveled by mere words.

Instead of writing it out, I thought about expressing our relationship through the formula of the Riemann Hypothesis, with the arrangement of prime numbers. Primes exist without a consistent pattern, yet within them lies a hidden complexity and meaning. Even if humanity ceases to exist, primes—no, more accurately, numbers—will continue to survive. When we walk into a restaurant and say, "Three, please," we naturally use numbers, but the concept they represent transcends human life. Numbers are more fundamental than language. Without them, we might be forced to say "pie, pie, pie" in repetition.

Even if language disappears, even if humanity perishes, numbers will always exist in the vastness of the universe. If we ever meet extraterrestrial life, it could be through numbers that we communicate.

The mystery and order within numbers may be a universal language shared across the cosmos, one that expresses both structure and the hidden chaos of existence.

'If my father and I had communicated not through words, but through the language of numbers, would things have been different? Would it have torn down the walls between us, connecting our hearts?'

'For 35 years, we remained confined to our separate corners, navigating the unsolved maze of emotions. This mystery... one day, it must be deciphered.'

To my dying father, my first letter:

→ ◇2, 3, 5, 7, 11, 13, 17, 19, 23, 29, 31, 37, 41◇

2 = W (The first letter of "We")

3 = E (The second letter of "We")

5 = C (The first letter of "Cannot")

7 = A (The second letter of "Cannot")

11 = N (The third letter of "Cannot")

13 = N (The first letter of "Not")

17 = U (The first letter of "Understand")

19 = N (The second letter of "Understand")

23 = D (The third letter of "Understand")

29 = E (The first letter of "Each")

31 = A (The first letter of "And")

37 = O (The first letter of "Other")

41 = T (The first letter of "The")

Decoded letter content: "We cannot understand each other."

The reason why 2 is W: "We" symbolizes my father and me, signifying that we are family. "W" is the first letter of our connection, embodying the once-shared will to be together.

The reason why 3 is E: "E" is the second letter in "We," meaning that our conversations should have continued, but they didn't.

Lastly, the prime numbers 5, 7, 11, 13, 17, 19, 23, 29, 31, 37, 41: These primes represented the conflicts between my father and me, illustrating the process of us not understanding each other. The irregular distribution of primes also implied the complexity of our relationship.

December 9, 2024 / Weather: Clear

I woke up early, boiled water in the coffee pot, and the scent of coffee wafting from the kitchen offered me some comfort. However, ever since I received that strange email, my thoughts have been consumed by my father.

I was about to leave for the bookstore but stopped in front of the mirror to adjust myself. I put on a black trench coat suited for the early winter chill. While the smooth fabric blocked the wind, the cold seeping inside was unavoidable. I boarded the subway, looking around at the other passengers. Most were absorbed in their smartphones or wearing the wearied expressions of people slowly sinking into the darkness of winter. The man beside me was reading a Google news article, while the woman across from me had her earphones in. No one seemed to care about one another, all trapped in their own worlds.

I began to wonder if these people, like me, lived their lives ignoring their emotions. As the train neared my stop, the warmth inside felt even more frigid.

I tightened my coat collar. People still did not look my way. People don't care about others. Had my father also been ignored by someone while he was out working to provide for us?

When I entered the bookstore, the shelves packed with books greeted me—or rather, perhaps they pushed me away.

Though the books stood firm in their places, I was merely an intruder among them. I walked slowly, letting my eyes wander across the different titles. Familiar names caught my attention: At the End of Loneliness, The Aesthetics of Solitude, What It Means to Be Alone, and Loneliness in the Crowd. Just by glancing at the titles, a cold, heavy feeling arose within me. My fingers brushed lightly along the spines of the books, hesitating on which one to pick, but my hand found no resting place.

After a while, my hand stopped on The Meaning of Solitude, a popular book that straddled the line between psychology and philosophy, digging deep into the root of modern loneliness and isolation. As I pulled it from the shelf and opened it, the words seemed to speak directly to me.

"Humans are all solitary beings."

"Even when surrounded by others, we still feel loneliness—that's the essence of being human."

I sat down on a nearby chair and continued reading. The book elaborated on loneliness, delving into research and statistics, showing how deeply it permeated modern life.

'Did Father ever read this book? Or perhaps he endured loneliness in his own way?'

I closed the book and looked up, scanning the bookstore again. People were still engrossed in their own worlds, carefully selecting books. In a world where loneliness is so pervasive, are we truly alone? Or are we merely living by accepting the fact that we all are?

By now, my watch hands pointed to 2:00 p.m. I quickly left the bookstore and stood in front of the crosswalk. On my way to meet an old colleague.

I took out my smartphone and turned on GPS. "In a few meters, you will reach your destination."

I knew exactly where I was. At least in a physical sense, I existed here. The GPS always pinpointed my location accurately, as if losing my way in the world were impossible.

But inside, it was different. The physical coordinates told me where I was, but my emotional coordinates? They were nowhere to be found. Loneliness gives no location. It simply drifts like a lost star in the universe. My body stood there, grounded, while the blue dot marked my physical presence.

This damned feeling, which no precise technology could measure, deepened with each step I took.

Father, too, must have followed his exact coordinates, commuting the same route daily, but his heart must have longed to wander far. Hidden in his suspicious coat was his own form of loneliness—a location I could never reach.

I stood for a moment longer, staring at the blue dot, then turned off my phone. The café near City Hall, where I arrived, was unchanged. My colleague was already seated, waving at me.

"Hey, Yeong-hwan. How've you been?"

"So, what are you up to these days?"

"Oh, just writing. Been working on something about my father lately, but... it's tough."

He nodded but responded with the usual platitudes. "Yeah, writing about parents is hard. Especially Korean fathers—always so silent, solving everything on their own."

He wasn't wrong. Yet, I couldn't help but wonder how much emotion had been suppressed beneath that silence.

"That silence... it's something."

As he walked the same path to work every morning, as the GPS precisely led him to his destination, what awaited him at the end of that path? Surely, he too had his own uncharted errors in his coordinates.

I thought about it for a while, then took a sip of coffee. My colleague kept talking, but none of it reached my ears. Even if I listened, it would just be superficial chatter.

'Ah... I guess my conversations with Father were no different.'

After saying our goodbyes, I stepped outside. Whatever we had just talked about, I wouldn't remember it later. And to him, I would fade from memory soon enough. As Schopenhauer said, human relationships are merely a pendulum swinging between isolation and noise. In others, we seek fleeting comfort and solace, but it's like trying to fill an insatiable hunger. No matter how deep the friendship, it withers with time, and the effort to explain and be understood is nothing more than an exhausting endeavor. With age, I've come to realize how futile relationships can be. The act of exchanging emotions with others is as fleeting as dust in the universe. In the end, we all disappear.

Outside, the air was crisp, and the streets were bustling. I checked the GPS on my phone again—my location was pinpointed, clear as day. Yet, like Father's path of the heart, I too had no idea where I was truly heading.

I walked aimlessly for a while, then made my way back home. Sitting at my desk, I tried to move my fingers to write a few more lines, but my hand wouldn't cooperate. Once again, Father's shadow loomed large in my mind. The worn coat he always wore—it kept returning to me.

That coat didn't just carry the passage of time; it seemed to hold his entire life within its fabric. What secrets were hidden beneath that faded cloth?

Just like the dust settled on its shoulders, it was a mere trace left behind in Father's life. I grasped the pen again and let my gaze fall on the paper.

'No. That coat was his shield. From the world, and perhaps, from us as well.'

I looked at the healing cut on my thumb, gently touching the scar. The pain from that moment had now faded, leaving only a faint memory. The red mark irritated me slightly, but it too would soon vanish.

Beside me, Sol, the dog, wagged his tail as he cautiously approached. He nudged my hand with his head and then began licking my face. His small tongue was warm, strangely stirring something deep inside me. I gently petted his soft fur. The warmth of his licks oddly brought me comfort.

Like the scar on my thumb, can loneliness eventually heal too?

82

Pain is an instinctive, physical response, but loneliness... it blooms much deeper within. Even if Father's coat seemed sturdy like a shield, there must have been something in the inside pocket that was left empty.

That night, as I watched Sol, all bright and innocent, I pondered what truly lay hidden within that coat. On a whim, I slowly lifted my own black coat. The weight pressed down softly on my fingertips.

'Hmph... maybe it's not loneliness or solitude after all.'

No matter how much I reached out, I could never grasp it, and no matter how much I tried to fill it, that intangible emotion remained elusive.

If he wasn't hiding something in that coat, then maybe I must solve this riddle from deep within myself.

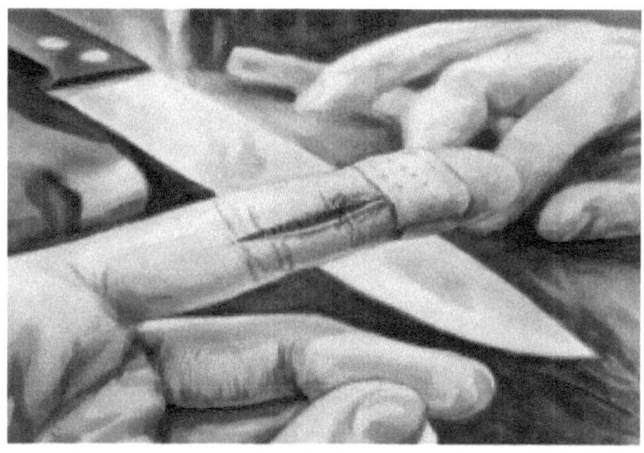

Chapter 4: Void

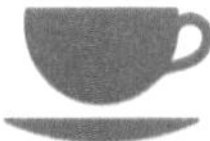

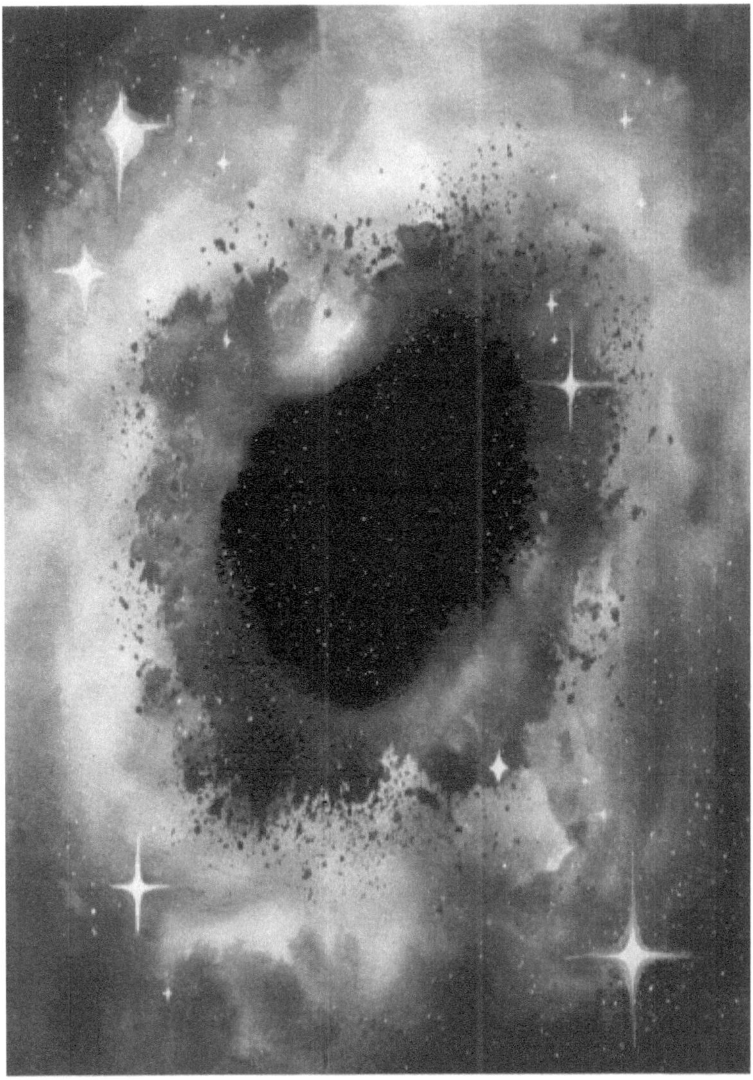

2024.12.10. / WEATHER: Clear

The morning sunlight faintly illuminated the room from outside. Sitting by the balcony window, I sipped my coffee, recalling the values of pain and loneliness I had calculated the day before. The emotions of anxiety, sadness, and anger lay coldly on the paper, transformed into numbers. But could these figures truly encapsulate all that I felt? Could this equation define me entirely?

"Sol" looked up at me from below, wagging his tail as if he wanted to say something. I decided to momentarily step away from the confines of formulas and numbers.

As I stepped outside, the chilly winter air swept in with the wind. The leaves had already dried up and accumulated on the ground, leaving only stark branches poking out. Everything was eerily quiet. We headed towards Hanbat Arboretum. Though I walked this path every day, today felt different—immersed in deeper thoughts. Sol trotted ahead as usual but suddenly stopped, staring intently at something in the distance, barking loudly.

I turned to see what caught his attention. There were just two ordinary trees standing alone, and nothing else. In that stillness, the vast emptiness of the universe crossed my mind. A space devoid of galaxies and dark matter, utterly empty in its essence. Even without anything existing, there was a strange sensation emanating from that void.

In movies, the line, "Is it good or lonely?" evokes both laughter and melancholy, but it's merely a social construct that forcibly combines the idea of loneliness. This loneliness holds the potential to connect with something or someone, allowing it to fill that empty space. The vast void, however, is different. It can hold nothing, nor can it ever be filled. Is it possible that we, too, are living within this emptiness?

A feeling of emptiness that neither loneliness nor solitude can define. The word "void" is difficult to articulate. As I pondered this, Sol sidled up to me and gently leaned against my leg. The emptiness I felt was starkly different from the warm presence of this little creature.

After our walk, I returned home, took off my shoes, and slowly walked through the living room. Sol followed me, trailing behind before curling up in a cozy ball, drifting off to sleep. Only the soft sounds of a puppy's breath filled the air, yet my mind could not find rest. It was time to return to my desk. This daily ritual of writing felt even emptier today. I resolved to type rather than write with a pencil, clicking my mouse. However, I felt lost about what to write, unsure where to begin. My attempts to quantify pain, loneliness, and these emotions had already formed into a semblance of a framework. But could I express the 'great void' in an equation?

"What is this feeling of emptiness?" I mused. "Is it something from a dimension entirely different from our own?" Pain could be measured in intensity, and loneliness explained as a quantifiable variable. But what about emptiness?

The universe has aged 13.8 billion years. How small must humanity be for such a disparity in age? Could that 'nothingness' imply infinity? The infinite, which cannot be represented by any number, may well be the essence of the great void.

I stared at the blank document on my desk, focusing on the empty space. That unmarked area might possess a purpose simply by existing as it is. If someone or something divine created this universe, why leave behind such a colossal blank? Or perhaps that blank itself is the essence of the universe? If so, what message might it be trying to convey to us?

Anything could enter that space, and anything could emerge from it. Thus, the blank is not merely 'nothingness' but could also be considered a 'starting point.' Isn't the human heart similar? When we lose love or miss something, that space becomes vacant. Pain or sorrow might fill that void temporarily, but eventually, what remains is yet another 'blank.'

We torment ourselves until that space is refilled, yet that space isn't devoid of meaning. Rather, it may signal that we are ready to accept something new. In Buddhism, there is the concept of "emptiness," while Christianity speaks of "chaos and void."

But filling that blank is the responsibility of the individual. Whether we choose to leave it in eternal emptiness or fill it with something is up to us.

What then is the opposite of emptiness? When I write, that emptiness always dissipates, and I sink into deep immersion. Every sensation seems attuned to the white paper and black ink, as if I and the world have fused into one. Are emptiness and immersion truly opposing concepts?

Yet, immersion isn't an emotion. Still, in moments of deep engagement, I don't feel emptiness. Nietzsche once remarked, "He who explores the depths must inevitably confront the void." Could it be that immersion is a process of exploring that depth? And when immersion reaches its conclusion, is it that emptiness lies waiting at the end, or is that very state itself void?

I paused, gazing out the window. Is the immersed version of myself indeed positioned at the opposite end of that emptiness? Or are emptiness and immersion in a cyclical relationship, placing me at a crossroads? Immersion might be a struggle to escape the void. Sartre claimed that human existence is 'nothingness.' Might the emptiness stemming from that nothingness be waiting for me at the conclusion of immersion, or is that notion void itself?

The human brain becomes confused when presented with multiple choices. Even in a simple café, like Baek Jong-won's 'Bbaekdabang,' the vast menu can be overwhelming. Having conducted experiments on pain, the bitterness grew wearisome. So, when I stood at the counter, ready to choose something sweet—caffe latte, sweetened condensed milk latte, green tea latte, iced tea... The options seemed endless. Over forty drinks listed, and not a single one felt like an easy choice. The more choices there are, the stronger the urge to delay the decision becomes.

There I was, hovering in front of the menu, wasting time unable to select a single drink.

Then, perhaps being deeply immersed in something means escaping the chaos of choice. If I could select just one option and devote myself entirely to it... That would symbolize a kind of liberation.

Is immersion ultimately about choosing one out of countless options and surrendering oneself to that? Are immersion and emptiness truly opposites?

Why did Baek Jong-won expand his menu? Perhaps he understood that even amidst chaos, there exists clarity at the core.

Until now, I had approached emotions as opposing concepts: pain opposed joy, sorrow opposed happiness, anxiety opposed tranquility. Anger opposed indifference, and loneliness opposed fulfillment. As I untangled each emotional equation, it seemed that all the complexities of the world bore a symmetry. However, reflecting on the relationship between emptiness and immersion, or emptiness and chaos, made me question the validity of that equation.

In emptiness, I feel like I am nothing, and in immersion, similarly, everything else vanishes aside from the object of my focus. So, what is emptiness? Is it a state devoid of emotion, or is it a state where emotions are all tangled together, refusing to surface?

On the surface, one appears full, while the other is entirely void; yet, in terms of the essential 'self,' both result in the disappearance of existence. Perhaps emptiness embodies everything—my emotions and meanings interwoven into that singular experience.

Two hours had slipped by since I settled at my desk. As I continued this recursive thought process, it became clear that "Void" represented a realm that defied measurement. I stared at the blank page, attempting various formulas to explain it, but no numerical value could adequately describe the void.

· $\text{Void}(x) = \varnothing$

When I first penned this equation, I found myself chuckling at the absurdity. Every equation must contain variables and constants, yet the Void equation held nothing. I tried substituting 'x,' but that, too, felt empty. It was a space that could not be anything. Just as the universe harbors a great void, humans too possess such a dimension. No matter how much 'love,' 'pain,' or 'joy' one pours into it, what ultimately remains is simply 'nothing.' It exists, yet paradoxically does not exist—an enigmatic realm.

2024.12.11. / Weather: Overcast, then Clear

Interpreting my father's emotions is akin to unraveling the mysteries of the universe. Like the vast void, he exists for me as nothing more than an 'empty' presence. In our conversations, amidst the fabric of his life, I found it impossible to discern what he was thinking or feeling. We merely coexisted, each respecting the boundaries of our own worlds. That unspoken space existed solely, and within it, a transparent barrier stood that I could not penetrate.

On the other hand, a black hole engulfs everything, consuming and devouring even light—an endless darkness. I have always felt like an outsider in his life. What did he truly impart to me? Though he protected me, his presence cast a shadow so immense that, as long as he existed, I could not shine my own dazzling light in that space. If he were to pass, would I confront a white hole? A place where everything escapes but nothing can enter.

The many reprimands he hurled my way, the misguided punishments he believed were lessons, could all come pouring out at once. What would I feel then? Pain, or a sense of liberation? I pondered my father from the boundary between the black hole and the white hole. No matter how I thought about it, he seemed more than just a vast emptiness. In his thirties and fifties, he manifested undeniable strength and presence in our home. Rather than being like the great void, his weight mercilessly dragged me down.

2024.12.12. / Weather: Snow

As I entered the exhibition hall of the municipal art museum near my home, the dim lighting made visibility a challenge. Squinting my eyes, I cautiously moved along the wall, scanning the array of paintings. Perhaps due to the bleak weather, death felt as though it lingered in the air.

A grand masterpiece titled "The Jewels of Plague" caught my eye beside the entrance to the first gallery. This painting exuded a desolate landscape, shrouded in a dark and mysterious aura, with the shining gold and jewels within Pandora's box seemingly symbolizing human loneliness.

"Is this truly treasure, or merely human desire?" A fleeting thought crossed my mind, reminiscent of the hidden jewels my father kept concealed within his coat. And perhaps, like this artwork, that coat might soon be linked to his death?

I examined the painting closely. The polished gems were interspersed with wrinkles and signs of peeling, representing a life marred by plague. This contradiction—the beauty interwoven with emptiness—served to amplify the loneliness inherent in humanity. It was the aesthetic of serene solitude.

"If my father were here, would he have gazed upon the jewels in that painting and felt a pang of loneliness?"

I mulled over the meanings of his coat, death, and the emptiness concealed within it. "Emptiness can indeed be expressed as a shimmering golden hue."

In this place, etched with traces of mortality, I felt the weight of life tangibly. If there were jewels of plague hidden in my father's coat, should I accept them as an inheritance?

I pulled out my smartphone and searched for the origins of each word. The term 'loneliness' translates to ◇◇ in Chinese. The first character, '◇', conveys the meaning of 'alone,' while the second, '◇', also signifies 'solitary.' In the East, loneliness is deeply understood as a state of being 'alone,' often interpreted as an existential reflection seeking inner fulfillment within one's own world.

In the West, loneliness is expressed as "solitude," derived from the Latin word 'solus.' It inherently holds the meaning of 'alone,' suggesting a rich inner exploration. Perhaps this Western notion of loneliness signifies a space for deeper personal reflection, evoking a paradoxical allure of discovery: "I can find myself because I am alone."

Next, the word "longing" is represented in the East as ◇◇. This term combines 'thought' (◇) with 'longing' (◇), embodying a painful psychological state. It captures the beauty of past memories while holding a tender sorrow for what has been lost.

In the West, longing translates to "nostalgia," derived from the Greek words 'nostos' and 'algos,' meaning 'return to one's home' and 'pain,' respectively. It expresses a fervent desire to return somewhere, intertwined with a deep sorrow for the unattainable.

Lastly, "emptiness" in the East is represented as ◇◇, formed by the characters for 'empty' (◇) and 'void' (◇), reflecting a sense of identity lost in a formless state. In the context of my relationship with my father, this emptiness also becomes a question about my existential being.

The Western term "emptiness" originates from the Greek word 'kenosis,' signifying 'emptiness' as well. It suggests an isolated state that the soul yearns for. While it could be perceived negatively, it also offers an opportunity for profound self-exploration.

2025. 02. 03. / Weather: Snow

Snow poured down outside the window. Each delicate snowflake, as it drifted through the air and landed softly within my room, reminded me of the warmth I sought to insulate myself from the chill of loss. Clutching my pencil, I huddled over the equations spread across my desk. They were not just numbers to me; they were a means of grappling with the dimensions of pain. I analyzed each variable that represented the thresholds of sensory stimuli and the constants of pain sensitivity, denoted by α_i.

I inserted the concept of pain into these formulas, meticulously documenting my daily encounters with it. I examined "anxiety," "sadness," and "anger," dissecting each feeling as if they were pieces of an intricate puzzle. At times, I simplified these complex emotions into more manageable models, attempting to capture their essence and understand their interplay within me.

In this dance of calculations, I sought clarity amid the chaos, yearning to quantify the intangible—emotions that my father and I had often struggled to articulate. It was a silent bond forged through the shared weight of unexpressed feelings, where numbers seemed to speak what words could not.

Week	Pain	Loneliness	Void
Week 1	3.5	2.0	Void
Week 2	4.0	5.0	Void
Week 3	5.5	4.5	Void
Week 4	3.2	3.2	Void
Week 5	6.0	5.0	Void
Week 6	7.2	6.0	Void
Week 7	4.5	3.5	Void
Week 8	5.0	4.2	Void
Week 9	6.5	6.3	Void
Week 10	7.0	7.0	Void
Week 11	8.0	8.2	Void
Week 12	9.0	9.5	Void

(Data on Pain, Loneliness, and Void over Three Months)

WEEK 1'S PAIN MEASURED at 3.5, while Loneliness lingered at 2.0. As time flowed onward, those numbers began to rise. By Week 5, Pain had escalated to 6.0, and Loneliness surged to 5.0. After three months, Pain peaked at 9.0, while Loneliness reached an even higher 9.5. Amidst these recurring records, a discernible pattern began to emerge. The numbers danced, forming a rhythm that resembled a melody; like a biorhythm, my Pain and Loneliness traced waves through the days.

These waves seemed intricately linked to my mental and emotional state. When Pain reached its apex, Loneliness would quiet down, only to spike sharply when Pain subsided. If I could represent this interplay visually, I could map out my emotions—an emotional landscape that would serve as a compass as I navigated the impending loss of my father.

"Waves...," I murmured.

I began sketching curves on a notepad, connecting the points where Pain and Loneliness intersected. That curve would become the most accurate map of my feelings. Just as the universe constantly interacts under the laws of physics, my emotions, too, followed a rhythm and pattern of their own.

Chapter 5: Wave

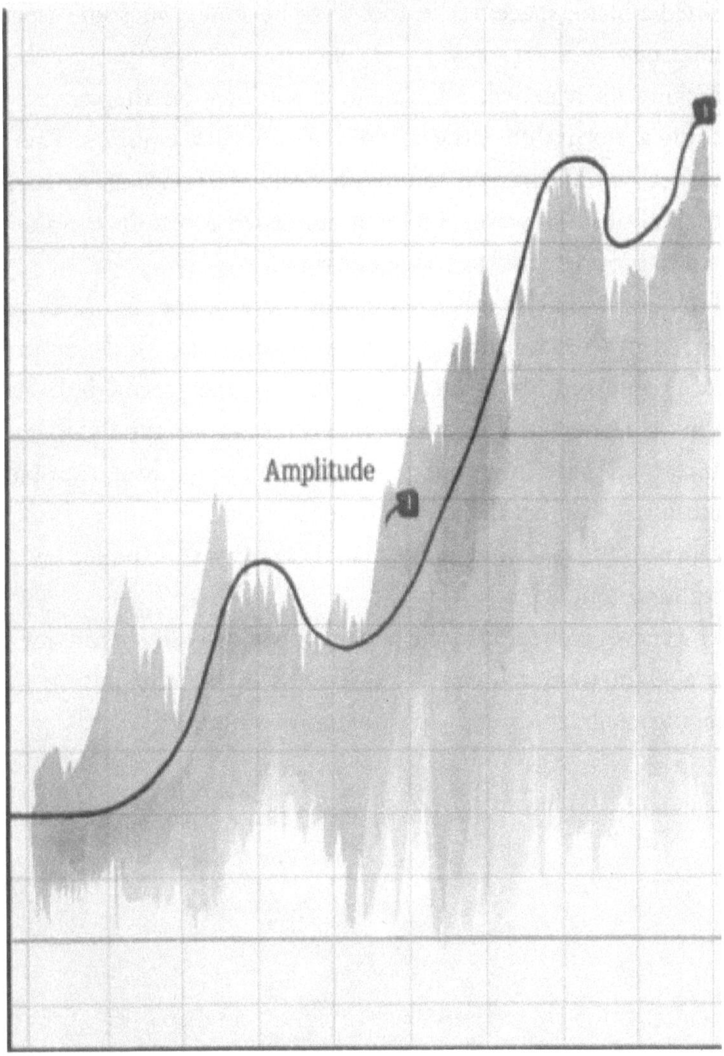

2025. 02. 04. / WEATHER: Cloudy

I stared intently at the numbers sprawled across the large canvas before me. These figures represented the Pain, Loneliness, and the still-unidentified Void I had experienced over the past three months. The values of Pain surged repeatedly, while the curve of Loneliness flowed with a relatively calm rhythm. The measure of the Void remained a blank space, yet it, too, must be conveying some aspect of my emotions.

Picking up a pencil, I began to draw lines on the canvas. Like sketching a biorhythm, I traced the waves of each emotion. Pain rose sharply, resembling jagged mountain peaks, responding intensely to external stimuli. However, unless it surpassed a certain threshold, it seemed to subside with the passage of time.

Loneliness, on the other hand, was more serene. Its waves gently enveloped my heart, calming me from within. The Void—empty yet pulsating—moved along an intangible line that seemed to absorb everything around it. There were no visible waves, but I still reached out into that space, my fingers searching for something transparent, something elusive that flickered just out of reach.

Once I finished mapping out these waves, I pulled out my smartphone. Click!

The curves etched onto the paper appeared vividly before my eyes. With a slight tremor in my hand, I pressed the send button in the messaging app to transfer the photo to my computer.

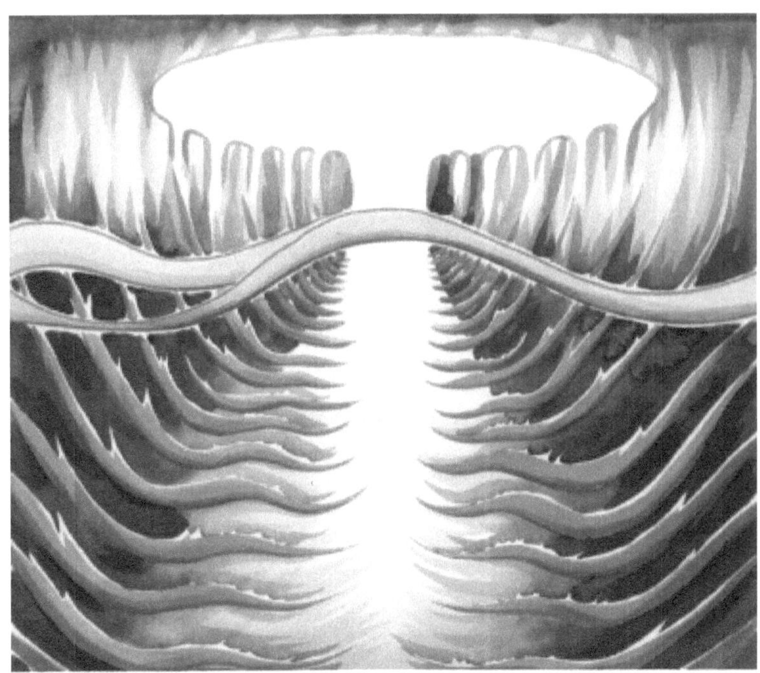

THE WAVE FUNCTION OF Pain

Pain is an emotion with fluctuating intensity, expressible through a sine function. I defined this wave as follows:

$P(t)=AP \cdot \sin(\omega Pt+\phi P)$

P : Amplitude of Pain (maximum value) = 9.0

ωP : Frequency = $2\pi/12$ (period of 12 weeks)

ϕP : Initial phase = 0

Specific formula : $P(t)=9.0 \cdot \sin(2\pi/12{*}t)$

The wave function of Loneliness

Loneliness is expressed as a calm and enduring emotion, and a cosine function seemed appropriate. However, when using Python, the CMD values didn't register, so I defined it using a sine function instead:

$L(t)=AL \cdot \cos(\omega Lt+\phi L)$

AL : Amplitude of Loneliness (maximum value) = 9.5

ωL : requency = $2\pi/12$

ϕL: Initial phase = 0

Specific formula : L(t)=9.5·cos($2\pi/12$*t)

The wave function of Void

Void has no wave at all, hence defined as: Void(t)=0

This signifies an absence of any fluctuations or emotional waves in the space defined as 'Void.' Every empty space is a reflection of this void.

Overall function representation

Combining these three emotions yields the following expression:

F(t)=P(t)+L(t)+V(t)

∴ F(t)=9.0·sin($2\pi/12$t)+9.5·cos($2\pi/12$t)+0

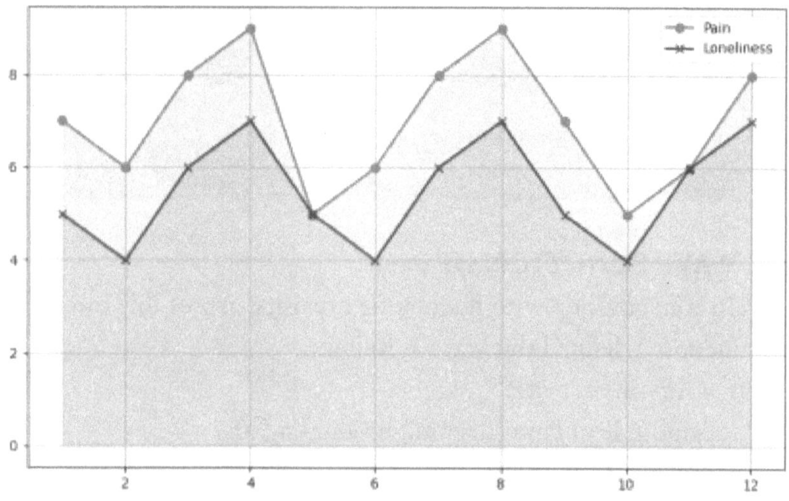

PAIN: A VIVID RED, with large, irregular vibrations

Loneliness: A smoother, more consistent blue wave

Void: A graph with no wave, a blank space

'Sol' had appeared from somewhere, quietly circling my feet and wagging his tail. I tossed him a piece of baby food while alternating my gaze between the defined functions and the waves. Loneliness remained tranquil. It flowed softly, drifting on the canvas like small waves on the surface of the sea. It made no cry, simply immersed in life, floating deeply in existence.

Pain, on the other hand, screamed with the crimson of life's source, blood. Its wail pooled in the valleys like echoes, leaving traces akin to the scars of suffering.

Pain, Loneliness, and the Void that exists between them create a strange balance that defies explanation. Was my father's coat similar?

I could not grasp his pain, nor could I feel his loneliness.

Yet the emptiness he experienced was perhaps not unlike mine. The Void may well be an empty vessel meant to hold the things that cannot be expressed.

He now continues his supervisory role in power distribution, traversing somewhere in Gangwon-do, yet within that coat, a gust of wind might still be swirling. That wind is close to nothingness. We all eventually fade into the void.

In the ongoing waves of Pain and Loneliness, might we ultimately converge into the Void?

2025. 02. 05. / Weather: Cloudy

The overcast weather continued. As I sat quietly gazing out the window, I suddenly discovered myself sketching the waves of stillness within my mind. The waves of Pain, Loneliness, and Void began to slowly fill my inner vision. The waves resonated with one another, each rhythm pulsating in harmony. It was as if a small universe trapped within my eyes shattered and then reassembled. Countless data points flickered across my sight.

With each passing week, I began plotting my emotions concerning my father, connecting them with dots. As the end approached for him, I could roughly predict where my feelings might land, yet I remained uncertain about the exact emotional storm that would hit.

Seated at the computer, I blinked as I meticulously examined how the waves on the screen moved. It felt akin to replaying a blurred film, frame by frame. In certain intervals, Pain peaked, while at others, Loneliness quietly submerged only to resurface again. I was gradually coming to terms with the reality that the culmination of all these emotions would be my father's death. I had to accept that it was the destination and conclusion of my feelings.

Finally, those waves coalesced, aligning into a single undulation that matched the metrics of all my emotions. My personal emotional map was complete. The tangled knots of feeling began to unravel, lightening the weight of confusion. Even the Void, once merely an empty space, receded into the background like a distant, indistinct melody.

The end was always tranquil. "Is this it?" I muttered, and just as I did, despite having confirmed, predicted, and mathematically demonstrated every emotion, another sensation of emptiness emerged, striking my feelings like a dimensional wave.

I pressed the print button for my unique map displayed on the computer screen. The wave graph—Pain, Loneliness, and Void—emerged from the printer. The representation of these three emotions, quantified and drawn as curves, was astonishing. As ink spread across the thin paper, the waves danced, revealing the state of my emotions. I carefully pinned the map to one side of the wall and began to examine the linear graphs closely.

Stepping back from the wall, I looked at the waves again. "Ah, would it be a bit lacking to have music missing from this blessed moment?" I mused, gently stroking Sol's head, who was staring intently at me from the side.

Now, all that remained was music that could harmonize with those emotions.

I preferred instrumental music without lyrics. Lyrics often seemed to impose someone else's intent or explanation onto my heart, which could be quite bothersome. I could only truly appreciate music when rhythm and repeating tones resonated deep within my soul. I opened YouTube and searched for the "Pachelbel's Canon." As the gentle melody flowed out, the maps before my eyes seemed to come alive. With each strike of the piano keys, the wave of Pain trembled ever so slightly, and the subtle curve of Loneliness swayed quietly in tune with the music.

As Pachelbel's Canon drew to a close, I switched to Beethoven's "Moonlight Sonata." The dark, heavy melody filled the room, causing the wave of Pain to surge violently. The once-calm curve of Loneliness held its breath, sinking deeply. When Chopin's Nocturne began to play, I found myself immersed in a sense of healing. The wave of Loneliness flowed gently within the graph, while the wave of Pain momentarily receded. The music flowed, intertwining with those waves, and I surrendered my entire being to the classical pieces. While music could not fill every void between those waves, it offered a temporary escape from that space.

When the classical music stopped, stillness returned. Hmm... somehow, merely gazing at the three waves felt lacking. I wondered what it would be like if those waves were expressed audibly, as sound, like the music I had just listened to. Since the melody itself was a wave, transforming these emotional amplitudes into sound could be rather intriguing.

If I were to express these waves through music, whose compositions would fit? Beethoven? His music bursts with energy and immense power. It might be suitable for depicting Pain, but it seemed distant from Loneliness and Void. What about Mozart? Upon reflection, his work is too intricate and balanced. My waves contained emotions that were a bit more chaotic.

What about Chopin? His melodies always held a peculiar emotional weight, imbued with a sense of solitude. If there were music that could encompass Loneliness and Void, it would likely be Chopin's.

Thinking of him brought a quiet smile to my lips. Like the sound of a piano, I wished my emotional waves could flutter and then gently fade away.

2025. 02. 06. / Weather: Clear

I moved to the room with the piano. The creaking old door cried out with a "creak," revealing the piano that always awaited me. Slowly, I sat down on the piano bench. As my fingertips brushed the keys, a chill ran through me for a moment.

I gazed at the paper I had brought and pondered the "waves of pain." How could I express that intense vibration?

I raised my finger and pressed the lowest note, the A key. It rang out with a deep, heavy tone. Even after lifting my finger, the echo lingered in my ears, much like pain, which doesn't easily fade away.

Next, I sought the second note. A sharper sound resonated from a slightly higher note, ringing out a clear "ding." "Ah, this is the emotion transformed into sound at the peak of pain," I thought, as each key I pressed brought forth that feeling, vividly surfacing in my mind.

Now it was time for the wave of "loneliness." I gently placed my finger on the F key. Slowly, very slowly, a soft sound rolled out, "do-re-mi." Unlike pain, loneliness creeps in gradually. Listening to the repeating echoes, I contemplated how loneliness envelops a person and flows quietly. When that wave settled, I lifted my finger to the C key. "Click," a light but solid sound. Loneliness always returns in a consistent pattern, remaining trapped in an endless cycle.

Finally, I aimed to express "emptiness," but it eluded me as a sound. I let my fingers hover in the air, simply gazing at the keys. I pressed into the void, exploring the depth of that silence. The stillness that followed the sound's disappearance was emptiness itself.

I took a deep breath and attempted to connect all the notes. Pain, loneliness, and the emptiness nestled between them. "Doo-wee," "ding," "do-re-mi," and the subsequent silence. The sound of pain echoed large and heavy, the sound of loneliness flowed softly, with suffocating voids piercing through at intervals.

Each note intertwined, and my emotions flowed like waves. It felt as though the hidden feelings within me were being drawn out one by one, exposing them to the world. The waves grew stronger, and the tide of emotions enveloped me deeper. Each sound struck the layers of pain nested within me, the vibrations permeating through my body and sinking deep into my heart. Even the brief moments of silence between the sounds resonated.

The transformation of emotions into sound, echoing back as auditory waves, allowed me to simultaneously experience confusion and stability. I took out my smartphone and pressed the record button.

As I began to play again, the sounds born from my fingertips filled the room, sometimes screaming, sometimes rippling like gentle waves, endlessly repeating until they vanished.

It was a panorama of the emotions I had lived through for 35 years and the flow of all my memories. The cold yet unyielding "map of emotions" I had quantified now breathed life as music, stirring my heart.

Once the last notes faded away, I looked up at the smartphone resting on the shelf. The sound stored there was a collection proving the flow of my existence. I connected the smartphone to the computer to transfer the files. With each blue bar that gradually filled, the weight of the emotions I had amassed added more capacity to the hard drive.

"Is this what musicians or artists feel when they finish a piece?"

The heavy emotions that had lingered at my fingertips seemed to harden, much like paint that has seeped completely into a canvas, never to spread again. Simultaneously, a certain emptiness washed over me in that moment of completion.

"Is this truly enough to express the feelings between my father and me?"

Musicians often exhale deeply after playing their final notes, feeling the sensation of a singular work emerging from their fingertips. When the last sound vanishes, what remains in the silence is not merely the sound itself, but the space it has created and the emotional traces it has filled.

The feelings experienced at the end of a long dream, once I finally reach that conclusion. The sounds I crafted with my fingertips, those waves transformed into remnants of my emotions, became files on the computer screen.

As the progress bar reached its end and the file transferred completed, I smiled involuntarily. The peculiar emptiness artists feel upon completing a piece, the liberation musicians experience after striking their last note, and the fulfillment painters feel after their final brushstroke—all existing within that ethereal emotion.

Finally, when those waves took form as music, it felt as if my feelings toward my father were fully realized.

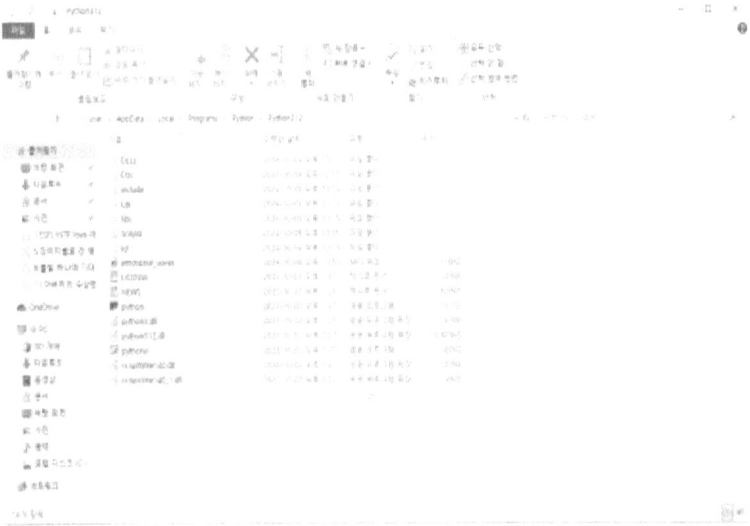

'Click' : emotional_waves.MP3

Chapter 6: Disorder

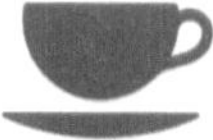

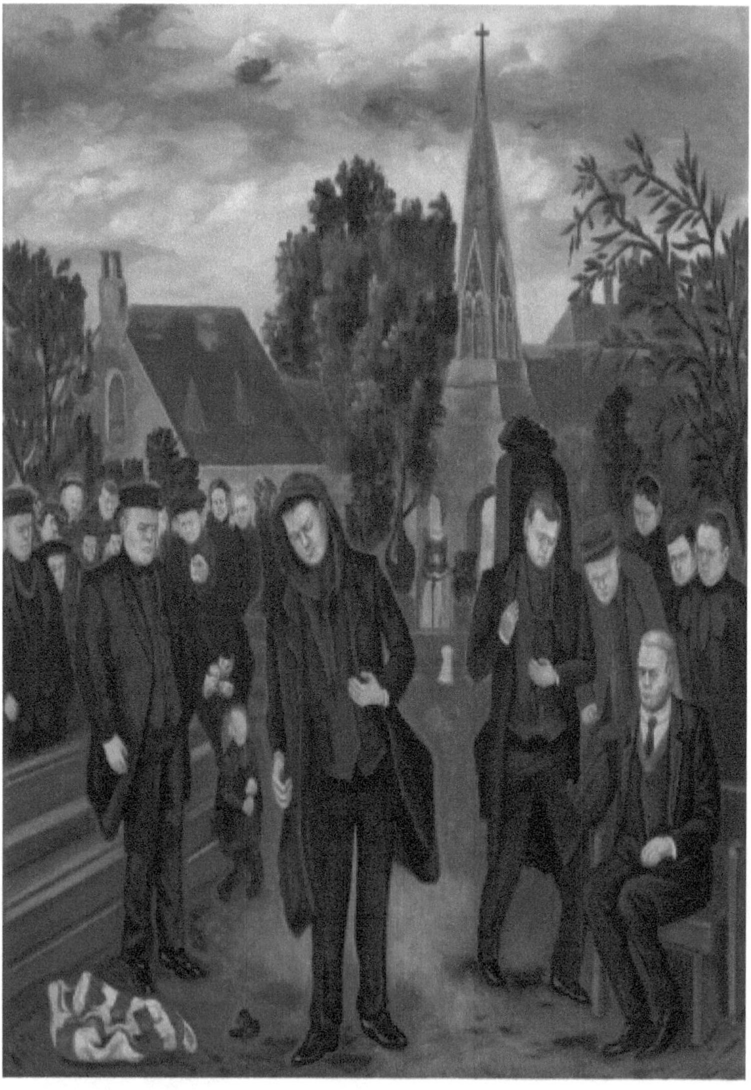

2025. 05. 22. / WEATHER: Clear

That day, an unsettling feeling nestled deep within me. Even the transparent light of the clear sunshine seemed tainted with an impurity of sorts. Yet, the source of my unease lay beyond the mere gaze of the weather. It was the behavior of our dog, Sol—every slight, unusual gesture felt intrusive. Perhaps it was just my sensitivity, but the silence around me was thick with an unidentifiable anxiety radiating from those watching eyes. The memory of a dream I had just moments ago lingered in my mind, haunting me. A lost soul had gazed at me and gestured, draped in my father's overcoat. Though no cold wind had blown, the coat fluttered faintly, and while there was no face to see, the gaze of that spirit fixated on me. As I cautiously approached, a familiar scent wafted from the coat: the stale tobacco smoke, remnants of a life that had once borne heavy burdens. Then, from within that coat, something writhed, almost as if it were alive.

This time, the coat began to move slowly toward me. Or rather, something inside it advanced in my direction. Fear gripped me. Was it my father inside, or something entirely different? The coat seemed to be reaching out to convey a message. Suddenly, a cold, unfamiliar hand shot out, as if trying to grasp me. Just as that hand made contact, I jolted awake.

As I quelled the tumultuous feelings inside me, my phone vibrated above my head. A name I didn't recognize appeared on the screen—it was a colleague of my father's.

"Is this Yeong-hwan Choi?" His voice was low and calm. Just hearing it foretold the inevitable. "Your father... at the university hospital..." he paused, a breath hanging heavy in the air. "He's gone..."

Waves of soundless energy rippled through my mind. An image formed—a straight line traversing the screen, representing a waveform. After a long stretch of time, that line finally ceased, cutting off all motion. A waveform with no amplitude, no fluctuations, waiting for me at the edge of the world.

I knew my father had already prepared for this moment. Death had become a task, something he'd meticulously arranged, from funeral expenses to hospital procedures.

I gathered Sol in my arms and climbed into the car. As the engine roared to life, the world outside began to unfold slowly beyond the window. The morning sunlight was sharper here than what I had seen from home, yet it felt cold. Sol sat quietly in the passenger seat, watching me without the usual wag of his tail, and I drove silently toward Gangwon-do.

Upon reaching the toll booth on the highway to Gangwon-do, I dialed my sister's number. A few mechanical rings echoed in the air before her voice broke through. "Dad... passed away."

In the stretch of that short silence, I couldn't fathom what thoughts were racing through her mind. Only a profound emptiness filled my own. I hung up and reached out to my mother. She was temporarily staying at my aunt's house in another city. Saying those words—my father's death—left my voice devoid of emotion. I couldn't tell how those words landed on her.

The void felt eerily similar to the concept of death. Both stood still in their silence, leaving nothing in their wake. Outside the car, the landscape blurred by, flowing along the straight road, with emptiness as my only companion.

I turned on the music. The sounds of the waveform I had created—notes encapsulating pain, loneliness, and the space in between—filled the air.

Upon arriving in Gangwon-do, a fog hung in the air like the dust settled on the road. As the hazy scenery sharpened into focus, the worn facade of the university hospital revealed itself. The building appeared aged and crumbling. Its exterior resembled a timeworn stone, faded and roughened by the passage of years, where time had imprinted its essence in the crevices. The hospital stood like a vast vacuum, silently absorbing all that passed within its walls, where countless lives had intersected with death. The thought that this was the place where my father had drawn his last breath sent a chill coursing through me.

As I stepped inside, a frigid draft brushed against my collar, pushing me forward. The footsteps of people walking the hallways echoed softly, while fluorescent lights above blinked rhythmically. Here, time felt as though it flowed differently. What must my father have felt in those final moments? He had left me with no parting words, no hints of what lay ahead. The journey from the hospital to the funeral home was long and silent. Entering the space he had prepared, I felt that vague unease from my dream solidify into reality.

The funeral home was dim, and as I moved deeper into the room, a heavy atmosphere pressed down on me. The gray wallpaper enveloped the narrow chamber, where creaky wooden chairs were adorned with cheap faux-leather cushions. Everything in that room spoke volumes about my father's character.

I entered a small waiting room that resembled a hotel room. A sign on the wooden door read, "Resting Room for the Bereaved." One wall was lined with a large mirror. Standing before it, I gazed at my reflection. As I changed into my suit, the fabric felt cold and oppressive against my skin. I couldn't quite articulate what it was, but something heavy seemed to constrict me.

The word "intuition" looped through my mind. What is intuition?

I had spent my life transforming emotions into sensations, methodically unraveling them through numbers, equations, and formulas. Yet suddenly, without warning, a feeling would emerge, something that defied logic.

It had happened in my dream, and Sol's behavior suggested a knowing beyond my own. Had that little dog sensed something flowing through me?

The coat I had seen in my dream, too, concealed something profound. It felt as though it anticipated my father's death. But this intuition resided in a realm I couldn't explain rationally. So, where does intuition come from? Is it a sensation, or is it an emotion?

That feeling seemed akin to a hand reaching into deep sand, searching for something buried beneath. "They say women have sharper instincts," I pondered.

I wanted to understand this intuition better. Tightening my collar, I pulled out my smartphone with one hand. I typed the word "intuition" into the search bar. Yet even as I read the definitions and explanations that appeared, clarity eluded me. The text remained trapped in cold logic. Synonyms emerged—intuition, instinct, sensitivity, and more.

Note:In Korean culture, a traditional three-day funeral, known as sam-il, is observed. During this period, family and friends gather to mourn the deceased, share memories, and offer condolences. This practice is deeply rooted in Confucian values and is an important cultural ritual in Korea.

1   [noncount]

a natural ability or power that makes it possible to know something without any proof or evidence.
a feeling that guides a person to act a certain way without fully understanding why

Intuition was telling her that something was very wrong.

2   [count]

something that is known or understood without proof or evidence

I had an intuition [=(more commonly) feeling, hunch] that you would drop by.

출처 : Merriam-Webster's Learner's Dictionary

유의어

intuition

명사

instinct >	hunch >
intuitiveness >	feeling >
sixth sense >	feeling in one's bones >
divination >	gut feeling >
clairvoyance >	funny feeling >

Oxford Thesaurus of English

REGARDLESS, THAT THING called intuition had distinctly led me here. After donning my suit, I took another look at my reflection in the mirror. The person staring back was just as I always was.

People began to gather one by one, and the first visitor slowly entered. They bowed to me, their heads lowering, but I couldn't hear a single word. My neurons were still tangled in the remnants of that dream and the strange behavior of 'Sol.'

In the room labeled 'Resting Area for the Bereaved,' I had affixed the wave graph I had brought to the wall. Using formulas, I marked the first point atop the undulations of that wave. As the guests came and went, I tried to measure where my emotions stood. About an hour later, Mom and my younger sister arrived in turn. Mom wore her usual heavy expression, while my sister silently gazed at me. After another thirty minutes, my father's friends began to trickle in. Some nodded in my direction, while others engaged Mom and my sister in conversation. What kind of person did they remember my father to be? Their recollections of him must have differed greatly from my own familiar image. They spoke of how dependable he had been as a colleague and what he had accomplished throughout his life. Their expressions were complex. There was sadness, yes, but more than that, it seemed they were trying to find themselves within their memories of him.

As time passed, relatives started to arrive. Aunts, uncles, and cousins entered, exchanging brief words with Mom, conversations that quickly dissipated into the air.

I had no friends to call upon. High school friends, college buddies, coworkers—they had all vanished into some distant past, far removed from the person I was now. It was said that at weddings, the friends of the parents come to celebrate, while at funerals, it is the children's friends who show up, but I had strayed from that norm. At some point, my life had become a solitary journey. Was that a choice I made, or merely a consequence of time's flow?

I remained trapped in my own world, writing while shutting others out. In that sense, the distance between my father and me was perhaps a shared trait. As the mourners came and went, I sat in a corner of the room, listening vacantly to their conversations. Few spoke directly to me, and even they probably had no idea of what I was feeling. Or maybe, I didn't even know what I was feeling myself.

I simply sat in this space, feeling the time drift by like a hazy wave. Reaching into the inner pocket of my suit, I pulled out a marker and placed a second dot on the graph.

2025. 05. 23. / Weather: Clear

As dawn broke and the mourners began to leave one by one, I remained alone in the room designated for the family. The lights of the funeral home flickered faintly, while outside, the wind hummed softly.

On the second day, the atmosphere in the funeral home was eerily quiet. Few visitors came during the early hours, and the space was filled with subdued lighting, cigarette smoke, and hushed conversations. A few of my father's colleagues sat nearby, quietly sipping drinks as they reminisced. Their conversation was neither overtly sorrowful nor devoid of emotion; it felt as though they were turning the pages of an old book, gently unfolding their memories of my father. I emerged from my room and sat with them, yet I found myself unwilling to engage deeply in their discourse. I raised my glass to my lips silently, only to set it down again without a word.

By three in the morning, the only ones left were my mother, my younger sister, and me. Feeling fatigue wash over me, I retreated to the room. I took out a file containing piano recordings and pressed play. The notes of pain underlay the melody, while the sounds of loneliness layered gently above. Where exactly does my emotion lie right now? Is it pain, loneliness, or somewhere in between? The graph I created, meant to quantify my feelings after my father's passing, seemed insufficient to capture the entirety of my experience. As I listened to "Emotional_Waves," the furniture and objects in the funeral home seemed to shimmer like a mirage, endlessly writhing. My emotions and my father's memories were entwined in the same ethereal dance.

Before long, my eyelids grew heavy. I nestled into the blanket spread across the floor, and the piano's sound enveloped me, gradually fading away. I repeatedly pondered, Where is my emotion right now?but soon those thoughts too faded into a vague slumber, much like a straight line within a wave.

Morning dawned, the sunlight growing ever brighter. The light filtering through the window cast a faint glow in our room. On my way to the bathroom, I caught sight of the adjacent VIP room. It was a world entirely apart from my own. The entrance to that room was littered with haphazardly discarded shoes, and the air was filled with the sounds of heavy footsteps and a constant stream of mourners.

Inside, the family and attendees wept, shouted, and remained engulfed in sorrow, their tears flowing unceasingly.

Are they truly grieving, or are they merely confronting the immense reality of death?What exactly is the nature of their sorrow?It must stem from the uncertainty of how their remaining lives will unfold, leaving them trembling with anxiety.

After using the restroom, I passed by the adjacent room again, and their wailing resounded loudly in my ears. Paying them no mind, I returned to our family's designated area and marked another small point on my graph.

2025. 05. 24. / Weather: Clear

The final day dawned bright and clear. The awkward and heavy atmosphere of the past two days was drawing to a close. Only the last rites of cremation and burial remained. I felt little burden in following the plans my father had set in place.

In the early morning light, as we drove toward the crematorium, my mother and younger sister gazed silently out the window. I rested my hands on the steering wheel, feeling no urge to speak, nor any desire to engage in conversation. The three days of mourning felt like being pushed through a long, surreal dream.

The crematorium was quiet and clean. As directed, the procedures unfolded swiftly and succinctly. When the staff prompted us to say our final goodbyes, we bowed our heads for a moment.

When I looked up, I saw my father's cold body before me. He lay there on the chilling floor, completely detached from the passage of time, separated from the world. His face bore little resemblance to the strong-willed authority I had known. Instead, it wore an expression of peace that offered me no comfort, like a mere shell devoid of life. A profound distance lingered beneath that unfamiliar calm.

The truth was, I had neither disrespected him nor felt neglected by him. We were simply closed off from one another. Not being accustomed to expressing emotions, I found no sorrow or sense of loss in his death.

My father had been a figure who raised me as if I were a monster, and I felt like a mere existence incapable of perceiving even a single emotion he had left behind. We were monsters who never dipped our feet into each other's worlds. His death was merely another event in a long string of happenings.

As I forced myself to recall the past, the remnants of emotions accumulated over the years began to surface: pain, anger, loneliness, and emptiness. All of these intertwined with my father. Yet, for now,

I felt as if those emotions floated upward like light dust and vanished into the air.

As the burial commenced, several relatives and friends of my father bid their last farewells before departing. All that remained was to tidy up the traces he had left behind. Before returning home, I entered the family room and carefully peeled a sheet of paper from the wall. The graph depicted countless dots I had marked over the past three days, vividly etched into the surface. Folding the paper, I tucked it into my bag and glanced back at the room. Ah, I almost forgot my father's coat.

His coat hung lifelessly in the corner of the room. I reached out to touch the frayed collar. Initially soft to the touch, the texture of the worn fabric gradually seeped into my hand over time. The coat's wrinkles held the imprints of the years, carrying the weight of my father within it. Oddly enough, it seemed smaller today than I remembered. With that thought, I quietly stepped out of the room.

We headed to the final resting place my father had chosen in advance. It was a tranquil spot at the base of a quiet mountain, where only the sound of the wind could be heard. I wondered why he had chosen this place, but I found no answer. Perhaps, for him, it held no significance whatsoever. He might have simply opted for the most economical and practical choice available. Considering my father's character, that answer felt the most fitting.

With the confusing procedures behind us, we began the journey home.

In the car, only the sound of "Sol's" breath filled the air. Outside, the scenery passed by slowly. And so, it all came to an end for both my father and me.

Chapter 7: Time

2025. 05. 26. / WEATHER: Clear

I returned home and spent the entire day resting without a single thought. The next morning, I pulled out the paper I had tucked away in my bag: the wave graph, the dots I had recorded during the funeral. It was a fusion of the pain equation and the formula of loneliness.

I needed to analyze where I stood in the emotional wave of my father's death, given the calculated amplitude of my feelings. In hindsight, I might have known all along. Ultimately, that wave was not as significant as I had expected. The amplitude on the first day was limited, and there was little fluctuation. This time, instead of playing the keyboard, I converted it directly to piano sounds using Python. Then, I played the music.

The melody flowed from the emotional wave I had created. Remembering the record of the first night, I recalled the exact time: 3:45 AM. At that moment, my feelings must have been located at some point on that wave. "This is where I fit." Within the blend of piano notes and white noise, I searched for my emotions. Yet, to my surprise, they weren't substantial. It was as if they remained within the boundaries I had predicted; the amplitude of that wave was low. My emotions, like silent waves on a calm sea, moved quietly without making any noise.

There was neither pain nor loneliness. And not a single hint of sadness surfaced. What had my father's death left me with? I turned off the monitor, which had grown cold, and lay down. Just like that, it was over.

2025. 05. 27. / Weather: Rain

For some reason, I craved to hear that sound a little longer. I couldn't precisely articulate why, but I felt there might be something more hidden within the reverberations. Moreover, the dots marked on the graph had shown irregular amplitudes since the second day of the funeral. If that was the case, perhaps the sound was uneven as well. The realization that the sound was imperfect made me want to listen even more intently.

I turned on my computer and pressed the play button. Again, the first few seconds were serene. However, suddenly, the amplitude began to fluctuate erratically, and unexpected static started to creep in. White noise—a chaotic sound I had never anticipated surged like a tide. Random and sharp waves filled my ears, and in that moment, no emotion crystallized in my mind. Only confusion existed.

I quickly converted the wave into a function. I displayed the graph and observed its shape, but it did not follow any consistent pattern. There was no steady amplitude, and the size varied unpredictably. It was as if it mocked me, moving chaotically. What was this emotion? My thoughts raced. My mindset, which relied on rules, patterns, and logic, crumbled in the face of this chaos.

I attempted to catch my breath, but even my breathing felt irregular. Was this sadness? Anxiety? I felt as if I had fallen alone onto some unknown land.

Footnotes: White Noise:The mention of "white noise" in the narrative symbolizes confusion and emotional turmoil, which can resonate with readers from different cultural backgrounds. In many cultures, such sounds represent overwhelming feelings or chaos, especially in times of distress.

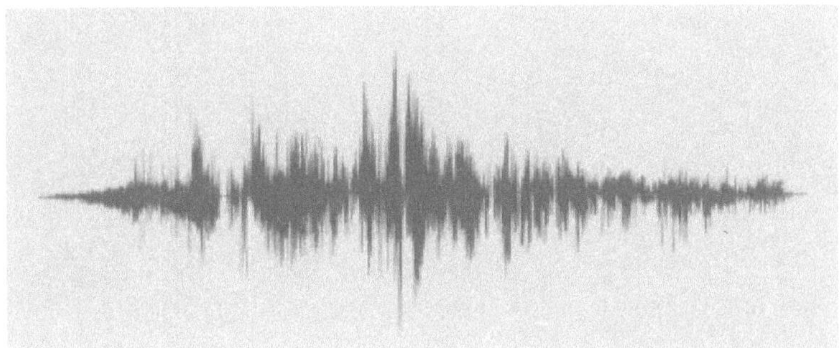

PC > 로컬 디스크 (C:) > Users > user > AppData > Local > Programs > Python > Python312

이름	수정한 날짜	유형	크기
DLLs	2024-10-09 오후 10:15	파일 폴더	
Doc	2024-10-09 오후 10:15	파일 폴더	
include	2024-10-09 오후 10:14	파일 폴더	
Lib	2024-10-09 오후 10:15	파일 폴더	
libs	2024-10-09 오후 10:15	파일 폴더	
Scripts	2024-10-09 오후 10:58	파일 폴더	
share	2024-10-09 오후 10:58	파일 폴더	
tcl	2024-10-09 오후 10:15	파일 폴더	
emotional_waves	2024-10-09 오후 10:50	MP3 파일	118KB
emotional_waves_with_noise	2024-10-09 오후 11:18	MP3 파일	0KB
LICENSE	2023-10-02 오후 1:27	텍스트 문서	37KB
NEWS	2023-10-02 오후 1:28	텍스트 문서	1,626KB
python	2023-10-02 오후 1:27	응용 프로그램	101KB
python3.dll	2023-10-02 오후 1:27	응용 프로그램 확장	67KB
python312.dll	2023-10-02 오후 1:27	응용 프로그램 확장	6,809KB
pythonw	2023-10-02 오후 1:27	응용 프로그램	100KB
vcruntime140.dll	2023-10-02 오후 1:27	응용 프로그램 확장	107KB
vcruntime140_1.dll	2023-10-02 오후 1:27	응용 프로그램 확장	49KB

The Remnants of Emotions Transformed into Sound

THE REMNANTS OF EMOTIONS transformed into sound flowed out as white noise, emotions I hadn't even recognized within myself. White noise. That sound, piercing through my ears and stimulating my brain, emanated an ominous energy. It was not silence but the resonance of souls. Could this be my father's last breath? Or perhaps a voice trying to take him away?

At times, it felt like whispers from ghosts. It could be a wail directed toward my father—a cry from spirits yearning to draw him into their realm. But that cry was not a curse; it was an emptiness devoid of emotion and meaning. While I was sending my father off, had they been laughing? Or had emotions I didn't understand exploded within that wave?

Everything was silent, and what awaited at the end of that wave was nothing but meaningless vibrations. "Big Bang."

A place where nothing existed. In that void, energy gathered and exploded. Thus, the universe began. Stephen Hawking described the moment of the Big Bang, saying, "Something that started from nothing became the source of all." Was this wave I felt another universe born from my father's death?

Physicists describe the Big Bang as an orderly expansion. Within the expanding space, galaxies, planets, oxygen, microorganisms, and more each found their place, resulting in our existence.

Could my feeling of this wave be the same? Emotions, unknown to me, stacked up orderly, exploding one by one at this very moment?

I ponder the difference between the two. If the universe was the starting point of a journey to find meaning, then my emotional wave seemed to flow into an endless void, as if those who created the white noise were mocking me.

One thing is certain: it was a wave resonating at the boundary of my father's death. The emotions I had cast away, the last traces of my father, and the silent voices of those who took him away. Perhaps this was his final message. Could this also be explained by a probabilistic model? Irregular waves like white noise typically follow a normal distribution. If the mean is μ and the standard deviation is σ, perhaps I could find meaning within it.

$f(x) = 1/(\sigma\sqrt{(2\pi)}) * e^{\wedge}(-((x - \mu)^2)/(2\sigma^2))$ "Yes, the normal distribution is central in the world of probabilities."

Yet, those waves seemed to mock the very concept of normal distribution, scattering everywhere. I could not find any concept of an average. I recalled Fourier transform. Would breaking down the frequencies allow me to grasp the true center of this chaos?

Each frequency component whispered to me. Those waves weren't constant either. Disorder. Yes, it was chaos itself. "This might be a Markov process. Random and independent of the previous state."

In my mind, the waves split countless times, and I couldn't determine where to place them. No matter how much I tried to fit them into empty spaces, they felt like puzzle pieces that refused to align.

Footnotes:Big Bang Theory:The concept of the Big Bang, widely accepted in the scientific community, describes the origin of the universe as a singular explosion from a state of high density and temperature. This idea may differ culturally, as some cultures have creation myths that explain the universe's beginnings differently.

White Noise in Korean Culture:The metaphor of white noise reflects the notion of overwhelming emotions and confusion in Korean culture, often associated with collective grief and loss. Such metaphors resonate strongly within narratives exploring deep emotional themes, illustrating the struggle to articulate feelings.

Markov Process:The mention of a Markov process highlights the notion of randomness and the lack of dependence on previous states, often used in statistical modeling. This may contrast with the Korean cultural emphasis on familial ties and continuity, which could provide a different lens through which to view emotional experiences.

Each moment was thrown at me like a random number. A·rand(). But what is A in this equation? How large must that amplitude be to contain this chaos? I could not even fathom that value, for it did not align with anything in my heart. Thus, I could not place this wave anywhere on the map of emotions. No formula, no function could be calculated.

This void was not merely a gap; it felt like an abyss of unfathomable depth. A colossal amplitude that transcended emptiness shook me violently on the graph, leaving me teetering on its slope. It was as if an alien presence loomed over me, something foreign and incomprehensible. I sat before my computer, facing this wave, lost in thought. Was this also an emotion? Or simply chaos?

First Thought: Waves and Disorder

In quantum mechanics, the wave function describes a particle's state. When a particle does not occupy a fixed position but exists in a superposition of possibilities, we call it "disorder." Is this sound I am hearing also such a thing? Everything is possible, yet nothing is certain, and the outcomes are not fixed. That wave seems to ripple before my eyes. Is this confusion I feel part of that wave?

Second Thought: Entropy and Statistical Mechanics

Entropy measures the degree of disorder in statistical mechanics. A high entropy indicates that a system is unstable. Its particles do not intertwine; they simply move randomly. I pondered the concept of entropy while observing the graph. Did these waves signify high entropy? There seemed to be no rules or order within them, like particles in a state of thermal equilibrium, scattered without correlation.

Third Thought: Disorder and Absence of Correlation

I traced my finger across the screen, contemplating what disorder truly means. It represents a state of uncorrelated elements, a collection of components with no connection. The wave's unpredictable movements mirrored that. The sound I was listening to lacked any consistent flow or rhythm. Was it just noise? I briefly stared at the screen before lifting my gaze to the void. Was it merely sound?

Fourth Thought: Random Vibrations and the Meaning of Waves

The vibrations grew increasingly erratic, lacking a fixed period and unpredictable in amplitude. I attempted to follow the randomness of these waves. Yet, like life, which I cannot control, this wave mockingly swayed chaotically. I glanced at the graph again, and I found no emotions within it. Like an equation for emptiness, it belonged to an indeterminate realm. If I were to distinguish it from emptiness, it was endlessly oscillating in directions I could not reach, like a colossal wave devoid of emotion.

Time slipped past midnight, and the sky outside my window was dark. As time went on, faint light began to seep in from the distant east. Even at that moment, the four thoughts swirling in my head began to intertwine endlessly—waves and disorder, entropy, absence of correlation, random vibrations. I felt trapped in an endless loop of thought. I looked at the clock. It was already past six in the morning. That sound still lingered in my ears, and the waves seemed to pulsate in chaotic synchrony with my heart.

When I opened the window, a cold breeze brushed my face, revealing a tranquil dawn city. The people were still asleep, caught in a time before waking. The streets lay empty, streetlights casting a gentle glow, and the soft rustling of leaves whispered faintly. Unlike the disordered waves, this scene exuded a sense of stillness.

I rose from my seat and walked to the kitchen. As I brewed coffee, I gazed outside the window. Dawn was gradually yielding to the rising sun, and the sky transitioned to a blue hue, brightening slowly. A few birds flew by, and cars began to emerge on the road, rushing to their destinations. I stared blankly at this landscape, feeling my thoughts scatter.

As the clock struck 9 AM, the world outside began its day, indifferent to my sleepless night. The incessant honking of horns echoed through the streets, and people moved along, their routines unchanged. Yet here I remained, suspended in time, caught between the chaos of graphs and waves. Within that disorder, I felt an unsettling emptiness, as if I were missing something vital amidst the relentless flow of hours.

2025. 05. 28. / Weather: Clear

I realized that there were errors even in the thresholds I had established. But that wasn't all. As I continued to analyze the unstable vibrations against the backdrop of white noise, another truth emerged—a new face of emotion I had yet to understand. My emotional map could not express this feeling. The waves I had constructed were rife with countless inaccuracies. But the two insights I had gained were of utmost importance.

I thought of the Second Law of Thermodynamics. Entropy, the measure of disorder, increases inexorably with the passage of time. The universe continually becomes more complex and chaotic. This progression is uncontrollable, flowing in unpredictable directions. But what is disorder and chaos?

Deep within my mind, I floundered. Like entropy, my tumultuous emotions grew larger. In the sea of white noise, I struggled to capture this feeling. It was not simple sadness, nor anger or anxiety. It was something far more intricate, a fundamental chaos my emotions couldn't grasp. I grappled with that chaos, feeling it envelop me. What was this chaos, and what emotions was I truly entangled in?

And then, it dawned on me. This chaos was linked to the coat. My father's coat—it was more than just an old, worn-out garment. It symbolized disorder and confusion. It encapsulated the turmoil I had struggled to comprehend for so long, a turmoil my father may have never understood in his lifetime. His coat embodied his attempt to conceal, suppress, and forget his emotions amid chaos. I came to realize that his coat was the very essence of his confusion.

Just as entropy relentlessly increases, my father's life and mine too swayed within that disorder, transforming into indifference. Thus, perhaps, that very oscillation was the core of our emotional experiences.

The day after receiving an email regarding my father, I cut my thumb while eating a lemon. The small wound stung, but as time passed, that sting intensified. It felt as if pain was stubbornly refusing to release its grip on me. In that moment, I thought, "Indeed, pain doesn't flow away with time."

While other senses dull over time—ah, scents, sounds, tastes—they fade like shadows in the dark, pain doesn't follow that trajectory. Pain clung to me, refusing to let go despite the passing hours. I felt it acutely, as if my body were shouting, "Hey, you've hurt yourself; get a grip and take a break." It was an odd emotion. Normally, one would expect it to fade, but why did this pain deepen with time? Pain was a crucial signal for self-preservation. If it dulled over time, I might have ignored my injury until it worsened. Thus, pain sustained its intensity, persistently watching over me. Yet, I had overlooked this significant truth—what was I thinking? "Oh, how foolish I am."

As I watched the healing process of my thumb, I felt foolish for not recognizing the error in the thresholds I had established. Why had I overlooked such a simple fact? Perhaps I had taken my body's signals for granted. Truly, pain is an instinctive mechanism intended to protect us—a signal we cannot disregard, an unwelcome visitor that continually provokes us, yet simultaneously serves as our last line of defense.

The formulas I had constructed were the painstaking results of my attempts to chart my emotional landscape. But now, they seemed rendered obsolete by threshold errors and white noise.

I glanced at the pen in my hand. Once a tool that existed for my sake, it now felt like a cumbersome, useless object that could no longer help me find my bearings. "What good is this?"

A sense of doubt crept in, and as that emptiness enveloped me, I set the pen down. At that moment, the clock chimed, announcing 1 PM. All my worries seemed trivial, and my thoughts began to settle, giving way to weariness. I lightly lay down on my bed, reflecting that my attempts to establish a new time coefficient were merely another futile endeavor.

Staring at the ceiling, I wished for the emotions, each bearing their unique stories, to fade away. I let go of my emotional struggles, realizing it was time to face myself. Fatigue washed over me, and I felt the cozy embrace of my bed whispering me into sweet dreams.

Chapter 8: Memories

2025. 05. 30. / WEATHER: Cloudy then Clear

My attempts to uncover the connection between my father's death and the waves of emotion had all come to naught. The disorderly waves had left my psyche in shambles, and the emotional theories I had constructed now merely fluttered faintly in the realm of faded memories. In a positive light, I thought, "Yes, even if everything seems meaningless, there is still something to be gained from it all." Usually, such self-justifications would torment me from the depths of despair, yet strangely, today, I found a small comfort within that sentiment. Despite the erratic nature of my emotional waves, which at times swayed unpredictably, wasn't that in itself a valuable discovery?

From the white noise left behind by my father's passing, I began to listen to countless waves of music, searching for the lost rhythm of my own life.

One day, a melody suddenly brushed against me like the gentle flutter of a butterfly's wings. In that moment, I felt a deep intuition that I was returning to my original biological rhythm. A tranquil melody ringing intermittently from afar connected the threads of my emotions, morphing into a new wave that sustained me. As the new music flowed, the dormant feelings within my soul began to restore themselves, and once again, my essence vibrated and resonated with the world.

Yet amidst all this, I still could not grasp the meaning of my father's coat or the white noise that enveloped me, nor how they intertwined with my identity. Ultimately, I resolved to accept that I must live on without fully understanding what that coat signified for me. What my father left behind was also a wave of anguish. Now, every time that emotional wave resonated within me, I discovered a newer version of myself lurking deeper within.

The concept of time had always tormented me. In physics, time is likened to a flowing river, while some argue it does not exist at all. I often felt as if I stood on the boundary between the transient and the eternal. While my past memories spread like a tranquil lake, beneath its surface lay various hidden waves.

Sometimes, the image of my father would surface, yet I did not long for him. Like withered petals, those feelings slipped through my fingers. Placed in the realm of time that refuses to flow, I moved toward an uncertain future, yet when I glanced back, those scenes were merely shadows that had passed. It was perhaps for the best that the moments I shared with my father remained not as brilliant flashes but as vague recollections.

In this severance of emotions, I truly felt how much the intangible concept of time tormented me. Like water seeping between my fingers, I struggled to interpret my father's coat within the flow of time, yet ultimately, it too faded into the void.

Current: June 1, 2025 / Weather: Clear

"Hello? Is this Writer Choi?" A low, calm male voice came through the phone. It was the owner of the consulting firm where my father had worked.

"Have you finished sorting through your father's belongings?"

My heart sank. "Ah, I only brought his coat back from the funeral home that day."

"Phew... The rest of your father's things are still in his room. I was wondering if I should take care of it, but I wanted to check with you first."

My mind raced. Why hadn't I gone to the accommodation that day to gather his remaining belongings? Had I taken his last traces too lightly? It felt inadequate to excuse myself by saying I had no time to organize his things.

"I'm sorry. I'll head over right away."

Was confronting his remnants still something I couldn't bear? My steps toward Gangwon Province were heavy with a mix of curiosity and self-reproach. After burning the last of the pine wood, I draped his coat over the passenger seat. Could there be something left there that I do not know?

The scenery blurred outside the window.

Upon entering the accommodation where my father had lived for the first time, I was relieved to see it wasn't a sandwich panel building but rather a newly constructed studio. Passing by a plaque with a recent completion date, I noticed the clean exterior walls and the meticulously paved asphalt road. I climbed to the third floor. His room was small, just enough for a bed, a small desk and chair, and a kitchenette.

Light streamed through the window, casting 503 rays inside, and I felt an inexplicable chill in the air. The new wallpaper was stark white, yet an oppressive silence had accumulated within that room for too long. On top of the small refrigerator sat a can of Let's Be coffee, his favorite, and on the desk were hastily scribbled notes about electrical wiring alongside opened work documents. Standing amidst his belongings made everything hit home with a reality I wasn't ready for.

I should have come here once.If I had bridged the distance with my father, I would have had many opportunities to visit this place.

I slowly looked around, stepping cautiously as if savoring the traces he left behind.

On the bed lay the clothes he wore in life, neatly folded. My fingers brushed along the creases of a shirt, and without realizing it, my feet grew heavy. I wondered if those garments still held his scent and took a moment to sit on the bed. I began to drape the clothes over my shoulders, then approached the desk once more. I pressed down on the drawer lightly, and the old hinges creaked as it opened slowly. Inside, I found a small box. My fingers traced the surface of the box as I hesitated to open it.

Finally, I gently lifted the lid, revealing a worn wristwatch. The watch had long lost its life, its hands frozen in time. "Why did my father treasure this watch so much?"

This wasn't a luxury timepiece; it was merely an object frozen in time, its worn leather band rough to the touch. I sat down in the chair, holding the watch in my hands.

"Like time itself has stopped, has my relationship with my father been frozen in time too?"

Though the watch was motionless, it seemed to contain the moments we shared when I was young. Had his life of unspoken understanding and solitude been trapped within this timepiece?

Suddenly, white noise echoed in my ears. It was the same sound I had heard at the funeral.

"Ah! The white noise was the sound of time." A simple sound devoid of emotion or fluctuation. Within that noise lay countless unspoken words my father had never shared with me.

"So, was all my father left me just a stopped clock? Or was it a final hint to find something within?"

It must have stopped the day he was taken to the hospital.

I quietly turned the watch over, adjusting the stillness of its hands to match the current time. 4:25 PM and 30 seconds.

The tiny gears whispered in my ear as they began to turn. The hands of the watch slowly began to move again. As the hands sprang back to life, a subtle change rippled through the stillness of the room. Sounds that had been silenced now reached my ears, and even the air seemed to tremble slightly. The flow of time that had been stalled, or perhaps something that had been stagnant somewhere, was returning at that moment. I smiled briefly at the moving watch.

Is it possible to turn back time now? The hands had returned from the past to the present, but I couldn't realign what had already passed. However, at that moment, I felt I was finally attempting to reverse my father's time.

"The white noise was the wave of serene time I wished to revert."

I loaded all my father's belongings into the car and drove home. Solsniffed eagerly at the scent of his possessions, incessantly burying his nose into them.

December 27, 1989. / Weather: Unknown

This is the day I was born. What was my father like on that day? Was he happy, or was he burdened by an indescribable weight? For people of that time, having a child was simply a natural occurrence, a surrender to the flow of instinct. They spoke of childbirth as a blessing and believed that family was an inevitable construct. However, I see this as a misguided perspective. The philosophical debate of anti-natalism has only recently emerged, but I've long considered the idea of being grateful for life as a relic of a bygone era. Occasionally, I mutter to myself, "I wish I had never been born."

Especially since my family was not happy, and I bear a resemblance to my father's violent demeanor, I find myself far from the idea of marriage. It's said that temperament and traits are genetically passed down by over 50%. With my negative outlook and preference for solitary work over social relationships, the chances of my child finding happiness seem grim.

If we interpret this through a philosophical lens, the dominant emotion in life is suffering rather than pleasure. In this country, it's especially true. With serious low birth rates, the GDP growth is bound to decline sharply, and the burden of supporting the elderly through social welfare systems will likely fall heavily on the younger generation. In a country that holds the titles of the lowest birth rate, the highest suicide rate, and the bottom of happiness indexes among OECD nations, can I dare to pass on such suffering to my child? The weight of that responsibility feels unbearably heavy and cruel. It's often said that the higher the intelligence of the parents, particularly the mother, the less likely they are to have children. In that context, knowing the structural problems of society, it seems foolish to bring a child into this world.

Of course, that may just be my narrow view. But with this knowledge, if one is not affluent, how can they bring a child into this world?

I believe my father must have known as well. He must have been aware of the challenges that lay ahead and the responsibilities he would carry. His happiness was likely tinged with a shadow of profound responsibility. I can't help but wonder: if I had been born in a place that values free and creative education like Scandinavia... would it have been different?

Should I be grateful just for not being born in North Korea or some impoverished third-world country? No, such musings ultimately hold no significance. Whether I was born or not, the world was always meant to be this way. Any attempt to attribute meaning only leads to futility. And I still cannot fathom what my father's feelings were on that day. I have no idea what my birth left in his life. Yet, I want to believe that he smiled, even if just for a moment. For amidst that weight, it would mean he had at least a sliver of joy.

May 28, 1992. / Weather: Unknown

This is the day my younger sister was born. Generally, men tend to prefer daughters. Did my father feel the same? Among our family, she has the most gentle disposition.

Of course, the stubbornness of the Choi family is hard to escape. However, compared to my mother's negative and skeptical nature and my father's authoritarian ways—and then the combination of those traits in me—she is still relatively mild-mannered.

As I mentioned earlier, she excelled in her studies. Perhaps her good fortune lay in being less affected by our parents. Graduating from Sangsan High School in Jeonju, she entered KAIST, then went on to the dental school at Seoul National University, and as far as I know, she is currently in her residency. I can't be sure, though; I'm not close to her.

As we grow older, she may have changed. During the holidays, when I return to Daejeon, I hear my parents expressing their disapproval of the man she intends to marry. I've heard he's a patent attorney.

In the grand scheme of the universe, which has existed for 13.8 billion years, a human life is merely a fleeting moment. What significance can those experiences hold? In this civilization, aren't we all just novices? When things don't align, people divorce, and isn't that life? If fate unfolds in such a way, we have no choice but to accept it.

Nevertheless, among our family, my sister is the most successful. Perhaps because she is a daughter, my father has treated her gently, unlike how he treated me. On the surface, she seems to maintain a relatively calm relationship with him. When the moment comes for him to leave this world, I only wish that his burdens will be lighter.

August 7, 1994. / Weather: Clear

In the midst of the summer of 1994, the sky was clear, and the breeze was gentle. That day, we set out for the mountains. I can't recall the name of the mountain exactly. The trees brushed past the car window, densely clustered, guiding us to an unfamiliar place. Inside the car, my mother looked at me with a soft smile, while I reached out my hand to feel the wind that blew in from the outside.

My father quietly held the steering wheel. His face was, as always, expressionless, but there was also a reassuring steadiness to him. At that time, I didn't fully understand my father. He was always solid, a silent guardian watching over me. I was too young to comprehend the weight he carried.

When we arrived at the mountain, we took pictures. My mother sat next to me, hugging me close, while my father enveloped me from behind. His hand was warm, but I sensed it bore a weight that was anything but light. My father looked incredibly tired. At 36 years old, he was already feeling the burden of the world. I am now 34, and if my age were counted in full years, it would be the same as my father's age back then. I feel the weight of the world he carried, even just a little. My youthful days and my father's middle age overlap, and in this moment, he seems to be reborn within me.

In the photograph, my father appears strong, yet I wonder if there was always a shadow in his heart fighting against the emptiness. Now, I understand that emptiness a little more. My father must have already been carrying many burdens. The responsibility of being a provider for my younger sister and mother, the labor for the family, and a life filled with sacrifices.

Looking back on that day now, it seems my father was searching for peace in nature, even if just for a moment. I can still recall his softened gaze as he looked between the trees.

January 28, 1996. / Weather: Unknown

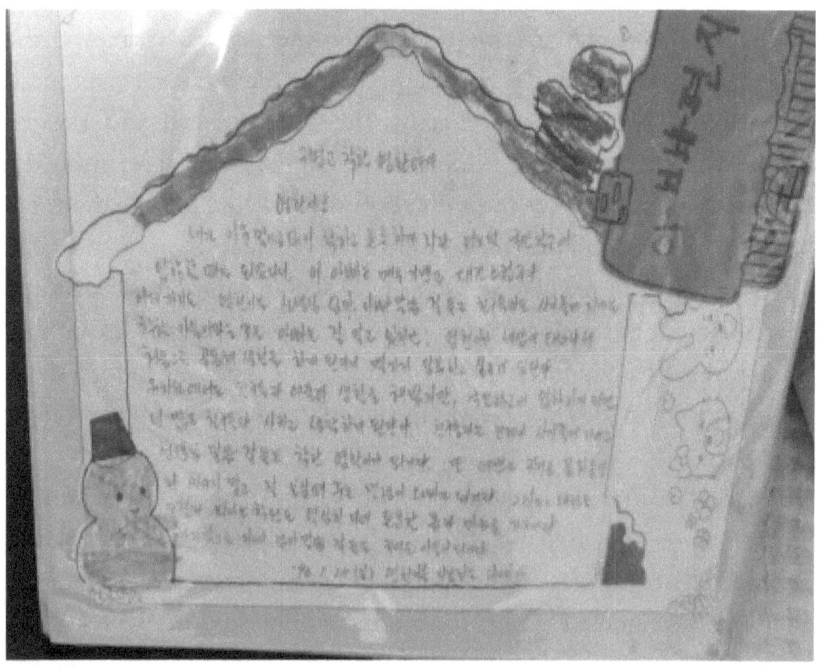

CULTURAL NOTES:

1) Childhood Milestones: The importance placed on milestones like graduating from kindergarten and entering elementary school reflects the value of education and familial pride in Korean society, often celebrated with ceremonies and gifts.

2) Written Communication: The practice of writing letters, especially in a parental context, highlights the affection and care that may not always be verbally expressed, contrasting with cultures where direct verbal affirmation is more common.

Translation of the Letter

To my dear and kind YeongHwan,

Yeong-hwan! It brings me so much joy and pride to see you grow up strong and well, and now it's time for you to start elementary school. I know you've been a good boy who listens to your teachers, mom, and dad, and gets along well with your friends. But since you're about to start living in a community for the first time, there are a few things I want to remind you of.

You've made friends in kindergarten, but starting elementary school means you'll make even more friends and spend time with them. Always be kind to your friends and listen carefully to your teachers. Also, please take care of your pretty and adorable little sister instead of fighting with her. Be a good big brother! Attend your Taekwondo and piano lessons diligently to develop a strong body and mind.

With love, Dad

As I rummaged through an old album, I stumbled upon a piece of paper tucked between photos from my elementary school entrance ceremony. The slightly faded paper caught my eye, titled "Dad's Letter" in uneven handwriting. In one corner, a small green snowman, likely drawn by a child, wore a hat. Within the frame of that simple letter, my father's heartfelt words were carefully inscribed.

"Congratulations on your kindergarten graduation, my beloved son. I am so proud that you have successfully completed kindergarten and are now becoming an elementary school student."

Faint memories from my childhood surfaced. I recalled the day I graduated from kindergarten and entered elementary school, my father looking at me while holding that letter. Back then, I didn't fully grasp the meaning of the letter. I was simply amazed that my father had taken the time to write something for me. But now, as an adult, rereading that brief message from him stirs a deep emotion within me.

"I hope you continue to grow and become a wonderful adult. I will always support and love you."

Though my father often seemed cold and stoic, the warmth and pride in his handwriting were evident in those words. Growing up, I hadn't always clearly felt his love, but that little letter made me realize just how much he cherished me. I gently traced the paper with my fingers, recalling that moment. During my kindergarten graduation, my father hadn't looked me in the eye, and our conversations were often stiff and brief.

Time has passed, and I have become an adult, far removed from my elementary school days. Yet this letter from my father freezes that moment in time, cheering for the young me.

I carefully folded the paper and placed it back into the album.

"How did we end up like this?" What could have caused the distance between my father and me?

The laughter and warmth of my childhood have vanished, leaving behind only his coat and watch. "Can this emotion be quantified? If so, how do we assign a percentage to sadness?" This puzzling feeling cannot be measured by sight, sound, or touch.

"What on earth could have caused this rift between us? Why couldn't I unravel the death of my father through an emotional formula? What does all of this mean for me? Why did I find myself hating and resenting you more as I grew older?"

Questions arise from deep within my heart. I once again recalled his cold expression. Sometimes, a faint longing would pass by, aching my heart. All of this resonated only within the depths of our hearts.

On the other hand, I envisioned Western customs. While comparing cultures may not always be beneficial, I believe there are lessons to be learned. In their culture, hugging and greeting each other with cheek-to-cheek contact comes naturally. This thought reminded me of a scene from a Korean advertisement. A husband proposes a divorce to his wife after five years of marriage. "We don't love each other anymore. Let's go our separate ways now that we don't have children. Sign the papers within a week," he says, handing her an envelope.

The next day, the wife approaches her husband and says, "Can we hold hands today? Before we sleep, could you kiss my cheek? And before you leave for work, you must give me a hug." She makes an effort to express affection, even if forced. And over the course of a month, the husband's heart begins to feel love again through her efforts.

Expressions of love can create a shift in the heart, and the husband genuinely falls in love with his wife once more. In a Korean song, there's a line that questions, "Can love really be achieved through effort?" Yet, love can indeed be sparked through intention and action.

Just from this, one can see how burdensome it is to live as a man in Eastern culture. Expressing emotions is incredibly difficult. I grew up hearing countless phrases like, "Boys shouldn't cry. They must be strong. A man can only cry on three occasions: the day he's born, the day his parents die, and the day he loses his country. If your father is gone, you are now the head of the family." (I heard this when I was nine.) For men, expressing emotions has long been taboo. As I grew older, even when I wanted to cry, I was told not to, and even when I felt joy, I was discouraged from showing a bright smile. This tendency is especially pronounced among those from Gyeongsang Province, where even some women display similar attitudes.

In South Korea, as one matures, the societal expectation is to hide emotions and to consider self-sufficiency a virtue rather than relying on others. So, hugs are out of the question; our hands linger in the air, empty. The wall of emotions grew thicker, leaving only wounds in between. If we had at least embraced like in Western cultures, perhaps our connection wouldn't have reached such a distant place.

If people don't express their feelings, they will never be understood—be it love, gratitude, or even hatred. Is South Korea really the best country if it has wealth? If one were to examine the phenomenon of upper-class disengagement, such statements would be hard to make.

Korean children and adults alike yearn to feel those warm gazes and the language of love. Yet, having grown up in such a culture, my father's life could only reflect that struggle. He was destined to navigate a world shaped by those times and norms.

Unexpressed love dissipates like the wind. The absence of emotion due to historical and cultural differences leaves me unable to fully grasp my father's essence, even as I understand his existence. I flipped through the album, one page at a time, lingering in the room for a long while.

2002.06.03. / Weather: Clear

June 3, 2002. The weather was clear. The streets were filled with the excitement of a festival, and the sky was high and bright. On that day, the air seemed charged with the collective energy of the world, as South Korea celebrated its historic first win in the World Cup finals. It was the match against Poland. I remember that day vividly, standing in front of the large screen set up in Expo Square with my father.

"Oh, Pilseung Korea!~ Daehanminguk!" The enthusiastic cheers and shouts of the crowd turned into a massive wave that shook the entire city. Wearing red t-shirts and waving the Taegeukgi, we were fully immersed in the atmosphere of the World Cup.

Before the match against Poland began, my father, as usual, spoke with a nonchalant expression. "Do you think we'll win today?" I simply smiled and replied, "I don't know. Poland is a European country, so they must play football well."

As the game started, the square was instantly filled with tension and excitement. When the first goal was scored, I instinctively looked at my father. Amidst the joy of people hugging each other, I think I saw a faint smile on his face. The game proceeded smoothly, and as South Korea edged closer to victory, the atmosphere in the square grew increasingly heated.

When the second goal was scored and the game ended in victory, marking a historic win for South Korea, I locked eyes with my father. Without saying a word, we returned home.

On a day in 2003, and another in 2015 / Weather: Both Clear

When I reminisce about my father, I cannot overlook my two puppies. They were the only sources of happiness in our quiet and gloomy household. I met the first, Hope, in 2003, and the second, Luck, in 2015. Now, both have passed on to the stars of dog heaven. The day I first met Hopeis still vivid in my memory. If I travel back 21 years, the school scene unfolds before my eyes. In the center of the classroom stood a green chalkboard, and the chalk—white, red, and blue—created a vivid contrast. During cleaning time, we would dust off the erasers against the wall, or we'd use a loud machine that went "Wing~~~" to make noise. At the front of the classroom hung the national flag and the school anthem, while, lacking air conditioning, an uncovered fan spun back and forth with a soft "Druruk."

On the left front of the classroom sat a hefty CRT TV, not the sleek LCD monitors of today, housed in a heavy yellow cabinet. With 40 students in a single classroom, there were 13 classes bustling with noise. Surviving the tough times of the '90s, we were on the brink of the 2002 World Cup. That day marked the beginning of summer, as cicadas began their song.

It was Saturday's CA(Cultural Arts) class. Back then, South Korea was just transitioning from a six-day workweek to a five-day one, and middle school students would attend school on alternate Saturdays. Classes ended before lunchtime, with group activities scheduled for movies, football, or bowling. That day, we gathered together in the classroom, feeling the fan's cool breeze, to watch a movie. Friends sat in front of the TV, laughing as they watched "Harry Potter and the Sorcerer's Stone."

"Wow, Harry is so cool!" shouted one friend.

"Right? I want to use magic like Harry!" another replied.

Before long, the clock ticked toward noon, and the familiar sound of the dismissal bell rang out, mingled with the children's pleas to finish watching the movie. I trudged through the playground toward the school gate. For some reason, my mother was parked by the roadside, waiting for me with my younger sister. Without asking what was wrong, I hopped into the car, recalling my sister's unusually bright face. That day marked our first encounter with cotton candy.

FATHER'S MORNING ROUTINE and Outings

Each morning, as my father got up and washed, Hopeand Luckwould lift their heads slightly. I think they sensed when he was leaving for work. At that time, they would wag their tails and see him off briefly before returning to their sleeping spots. But on days when he was leaving for work, they would whine, recognizing the moment he put on his shoes.

Mother: "It's fascinating how Hopedistinguishes between going to work and just stepping out. He stays calm when Dad's off to work but begs to be taken along when he's just going out."

Father: "I know, right? It's so curious. I wonder if he knows the days of the week or senses the slight changes in my behavior—could he possibly even pick up on my emotions?"

Mother: "Maybe the way you walk is different when you're going to work versus when you're just going out."

Father: "They're incredibly clever. To differentiate between my actions at the same time every day shows how sharp they are."

To my father, Hopemust hold a special place in his heart. More than anyone else, she adored him and followed him closely. Maybe it was because Maltese dogs excel at sensing hierarchies, but it was clear that Hopeloved my father more than anyone else.

Annotations:

1)World Cup Culture: The excitement surrounding the World Cup in South Korea is a national phenomenon that unites people across age and background. It's a time of national pride, often seen in public celebrations and gatherings.

2)Family Structure: In South Korea, pets, particularly dogs, often become integral family members, providing companionship and joy in often traditional and serious family dynamics.

3)School Life Differences: The description of classroom life reflects the traditional South Korean education system, characterized by high student numbers in classes and communal activities, differing significantly from the more individualized education systems in the U.S.

4)Cultural Norms: The conversation about the pets sensing their owner's emotions reflects a common belief in both cultures about the deep connection between pets and their owners, emphasizing empathy and companionship.

2025.05.03. / Weather: Cloudy then Clear

I slept in late for the first time in a while. I took my iced Americano and settled down at my computer. Regrettably, I still struggle to comprehend the feelings of others, and my own emotions remain a mystery. The contradiction of living as a writer despite having scored a mere 5 in the language section of the college entrance exam becomes increasingly apparent. I find myself expressing the imprisoned sounds within me with nothing but creativity and planning, detached from language and style. Just like my father's suspicious coat, I continue to write amidst the contradictions of the world. Sentences spring forth from my subconscious, lined up on the paper before me. Aware of this contradiction, I write diligently. Perhaps the reason I pen this book is to interpret that very contradiction with him. Today, I gaze at the tattered coat, unraveling the riddle of its secrets.

I force myself to remember moments with my father. While not many come to mind, the negative memories stand out vividly. Human brains tend to react more strongly to negative emotions or experiences;

this has evolutionary advantages for survival. For instance, after encountering a dangerous situation, one recalls it to avoid repeating the same mistake.

Psychologists argue that negative memories become more deeply etched in our hippocampus compared to positive ones. They recommend practicing a technique called reframing. This approach involves viewing negative experiences from a new perspective to uncover their positive meanings, a theme emphasized in various self-help books.

Moreover, the distortion of memories is intricately linked to the brain's complex mechanisms. Our brains process and store information through a highly subjective lens. Over time, past events are prone to alteration, and during this process, memories can become distorted by emotions or psychological states. For example, if anxiety or fear is attached to a particular event, the memory might be reconstructed far from its original form.

In this sense, my memories of my father are akin to shards of a broken mirror reflecting diverse images. His presence is reconstructed in my mind through remnants of old wounds and newly imprinted feelings. Ultimately, the distortion of memories is also our way of interpreting and accepting the past. The memories I hold of my father do not exist independently but are reflections of the emotions I harbor, constantly reshaped by the flow of my personal feelings.

When I attempt to reassemble the pieces of this mirror, it would be nice if they could reform positively. Yet I often lean towards a somewhat negative and skeptical disposition. Therefore, perhaps I only recall his unfavorable traits. Surely, he must have had a positive impact on my life, yet why do those memories evade me?

The brain seems to intertwine with my inner anxieties.

Returning to the topic, as I recall memories of him, I think back to the time I was at my uncle's house. I banged my head on a flowerpot, breaking my glasses, and on the elevator ride home, I received either a slap or a punch. I remember the stinging sensation on my face. Then there was the day I rode my bicycle at the Expo Plaza, slipped in the mud, and found myself unable to move my arm, but I chose not to mention my pain at home. I likely feared he would react explosively if I said I was hurt. A few hours later, he checked on me and reprimanded me for not speaking up, only to discover at the hospital that I had fractured a bone and needed a cast.

In the car, he was always unpredictable. When the smoky, suffocating cigarette smoke wafted into the back seat, it felt like we were in a gas chamber. I think I lived under that cloud of smoke. As a child, I despised cigarettes. Ironically, I smoke now that I'm an adult. Children grow up mimicking their parents, and perhaps that's why.

When the cigarette smoke became overwhelming, it was usually on the highway. Even now, the sound of the radio triggers memories of that car, making me feel dizzy. The overlapping waves of cigarette smoke and radio noise often left me feeling nauseous. For this reason, that memory stands out distinctly.

Every holiday, the highway that led us to my grandmother's house can be seen as a place where we stood still in time.

"Why are the cars stopped on a one-way highway like this?"

My father gazed at the sky and replied slowly, "I wonder. They could just keep going. Who knows?"

That conversation, simple as it was, held profound philosophical questions. In chaotic situations, he sought to understand the reason. Perhaps the conflicts felt in someone's heart, or the separations caused by some reason, carried meaning in each of our lives. As our conversation meandered, we both tried to understand each other, yet in the end, we remained unknowable to one another.

Yet strangely, even while reflecting on my father's lack of consideration, I feel a twinge of guilt for being a poor son. He worked hard for me, but I often question how much I responded to his existence. The truth is, I'm a monster made up of emotions I can't even accurately name. What use is there in speaking?

In family relationships, if fathers or mothers had said "I love you," they might have also used two words—"I'm sorry" and "thank you." If they had, our family might not be what it is today. I wouldn't have become a monster either. Such heavy words—"I'm sorry. Thank you."

Like the traffic on the highway, my heart flows slowly, exploring the past with my father. I hope positive memories will arise, but part of me fears that such feelings might bring greater pain. In that stagnation, it feels as if we are still lost.

To honor my father's memory, I walked to the piano room. However, since he could never be by my side again, I aimed to express his memory through music. As my fingers touched the keys and the first notes flowed, the tremor of that moment spread through my entire being. With the second note, the time I spent with my father flashed through my mind like a panorama. An indescribable sense of nostalgia enveloped me.

As the performance continued, my emotions intertwined, and white noise seeped through. The disordered waves crossed countless times with my own, introducing unnecessary noise into the otherwise serene space.

After finishing the piece, I created a file titled "Memories" and recorded the song. Listening to the playback, I left the room and leaned back on the couch. My father's coat, my emotions, and the music layered above seemed to find order within a chaotic mess. Rising from the couch, I gently touched his coat. The cold fabric sent a chill through my warm hands, and countless secrets still lingered within. I slipped on that worn coat. An unknown sensation seeped into my entire body.

Out of curiosity, I draped the tattered old watch over my wrist...

<Epilogue : The Secret of the Coat>

I NEVER QUITE MATCHED my father's temperament. Though I don't typically believe in astrology or fortune-telling, Korea has a cultural belief in the "animal zodiac," which holds that a person's character and fate are determined by their birth year according to the twelve animals of the zodiac. Among these concepts, the most striking is that of "conflict" (◇◇). This term describes a relationship where energies clash and collide. I belong to the snake zodiac, while my father is a pig, which is classified as a "Sahai conflict" (◇◇◇◇)—the most extreme form of opposition.

Cultural Notes:Zodiac Beliefs: The concept of zodiac signs (◇) in Korea plays a significant role in understanding personality and relationships, which may not resonate with Western cultural norms.

In Korea, the differences in temperament between parents and children, or conflicts between lovers, are often explained through zodiac signs. It's said that when a snake and a pig are together, mental and psychological conflicts deepen, potentially leading to mental illness. The snake struggles to comprehend the pig, while the pig finds the snake's complex psyche utterly unfathomable. Each time I think of these zodiac signs, I wonder if this fortune-telling could unravel the knot in our relationship. My father and I have lived as if we were in separate worlds, our emotional exchanges severed. Perhaps the conflicts between us arise not from differing opinions, but naturally, as a result of the laws of the universe surrounding us. The dissonance between us was as clear as the direction from which the wind blows, yet I could not grasp why it blew that way or what reason lay behind it.

Raising a child with a different temperament must be an arduous task for any parent. It seems that not just my father, but many fathers in Korea wear a cold coat. Beneath that coat are fragments of love left behind, preserved alongside smiles, yet we are unaccustomed to stripping away that outer layer. Fathers of the past were not the same as contemporary fathers; they were not friends. They couldn't share their worries or sorrows with others. Instead, they appeared like clumsy mathematicians grappling with their emotions. Their ways of expression and love were like that. If we do not understand their ways, they remain mere meaningless symbols, like unsolvable equations.

During our formative years, conversations with my father grew intuitively distant, resembling the uncertainty principle. My mother and father never ceased their shouting. Whenever I attempted to speak, he would close his eyes and shake his head or say, "That's just your opinion." As these moments repeated, I gradually distanced myself from his presence, and the gap between us widened. I sometimes felt as though we lived in different timelines.

Even when I was suffering, he would rarely offer a response. My desire to understand him only plunged me into deeper confusion. I found myself in an endless cycle of inner torment and contemplation.

Ultimately, I could not understand him, and the wall of emotions that stood between us remained unbroken.

My male friends, now in their mid-thirties, find themselves in similar situations, with about 30% already having crossed the threshold of marriage. They share a common wish:

"I want to have a daughter, not a son."

Growing up under such fathers, we lacked emotional connection with them, so they strive to alleviate that deficiency through their daughters. When they express, "Having a son is more difficult," I sense an unavoidable anxiety lurking beneath. There's a simultaneous pity and fear born from the awkward father-son relationship. They hope their sons won't wander in the shadows of their fathers, yet they also wish to hide their past wounds, fearing they won't be passed down to their children. They instinctively realize that without an emotional connection with their sons, they risk returning to the isolation of their past. Like a white floor left bare after the water has drained away, their hearts are filled only with deep emptiness. Moreover, I cannot even enter a romantic relationship or think about marriage. After several failed romances, I've come to understand my own issues.

I seek intellectual love while finding myself in anxious relationships. When my partner exhibits avoidant tendencies, my attachment intensifies. By the time they are weary of me and decide to leave, I find myself clinging to them with all I have—exactly as my father did. I offer material gifts as if to win their affection.

They neither accept those farewell gifts, nor do I believe I can reverse the situation. Yet, I continue to act this way. I know that material things cannot buy love. I worry, too, about my inability to control my anger. A monster resides within me. My rebellious nature, along with antisocial behaviors, has rooted itself deep within my heart, stemming from his emotional violence. Despite my efforts to change this stubborn, often violent tendency, the same mistakes keep recurring. "There are various masks hidden within me, and every time a repressed self emerges, it fills me with fear and dread."

I acknowledge that he fulfilled his responsibilities. Yet, I do not love him. No, I do not even like him. In my memory, my father's coat still hangs over my shoulders. This coat conceals the wounds of the past, like a thread of fate that is both tough and tenacious.

Korean fathers undoubtedly sacrifice themselves for their families, devoting their lives to them. They put on heavy coats and head to work, enduring sacrifices that cut to the bone for the peace of their homes. However, sons can hardly comprehend the weight of that sacrifice. They live as pitiful beings, ignorant of the complex issue of 'emotional bonds,' carrying the burden of responsibility while becoming perpetrators of emotional neglect.

Today, the issues of low birth rates in Korea are tangled in a web of high real estate prices, a lack of philosophy, and the phenomenon of women entering the workforce, among others, yet no one dares to mention these problems. No one speaks about why Korea is emotionally deficient. The phrase, "In our time, it was that kind of era," is understandable but provides no comfort and offers no solutions for the future.

These days, my friends look to Western books for answers on new parenting styles. "This way, you can be a friendlier father," they say.

The changes in young Asian fathers are quite positive. In the silence that once marked conversations of the past, today's fathers strive to embrace their children with loving words and hugs. If I were to ask,

"Did we love our fathers?" only a handful of sons could answer, "Yes." What is it that makes it so difficult for us to understand the essence of fatherhood?

Even while writing a book in search of the meaning of the word 'father,' I continue to wander. Amid this confusion, my love for my father remains tangled in ambivalence, never revealing its true form. The only part I can infer is this: Father, you were not just a man; you were merely an imperfect human being. I understand that you, too, were struggling to keep a family together as a father. The weight of life pressed down on your shoulders, and because of that, your expression was always rigid.

Behind that rigidity, I know there lurked pain and anxiety you could never reveal to anyone. You pretended to be strong, yet deep down, you knew how hard it was to fight against the world. And you did not need to bear that weight simply because you were a man.

Once, I wanted to gauge the weight of that coat. However, you were always clumsy with love, so I hesitated, turning back in the process. The weight I could never measure did not ease my heart.

You, a flawed person, and your inability to admit that flaw left scars in our relationship.

"You were an imperfect being, just like me."

My feelings towards you were a continuous contradiction. Your agony sometimes blended into my own heart, yet at the same time, I could not fully comprehend the pain you endured. You always seemed so strong that I could not see your true self behind that façade. To me, you were an unfathomable presence. As an adult, I tried to embrace your flaws, but that did not heal my wounds.

At times, I wanted to understand your struggles, yet that understanding only deepened my loneliness, and the oppressive words you spoke cast a long shadow. I wandered through the world beneath that shadow. Father, I cannot hate you, but I cannot love you either. The desire to understand one another evaporates like dust floating aimlessly in the air.

The pockets of that coat glow with a warm ember, quietly flickering. What you left me is not merely material; it is overflowing with the emotions you wished to conceal, the absence of communication, and the endless questions. I do not know you well, nor will I ever. Family is a bond forged through countless coincidences, yet we remain strangers to each other.

The relationships within families in South Korea are intricate and shrouded in secrecy. Therefore, rather than reminisce about that old, worn coat, I wonder if I might live by unraveling those secrets. Yet, the mysteries of that peculiar coat may never be unraveled, much like the complexity of quantum mechanics and the enigma of the Riemann hypothesis.

Secrets serve both as a shield and a key leading to self-understanding. That heavy yet light coat is an empty space of unspoken conversations between my father and me. Sometimes, as I stroke that coat, I seek to find myself.

"What coat will I be wearing when death comes for me?"

December 31, 2025, 3:20 AM

At thirty-five, I still find myself in a state of perpetual adolescence. No, perhaps I will wander like this until I draw my last breath. Life is an unending pain, a canvas on which I merely sketch various emotions. In the silent embrace of the early morning, when no sound dares to intrude, the words flow with surprising ease.

I open a YouTube tab while working on my manuscript. Gentle background music envelops me as the screen fills with messages of comfort. Beneath those warm sentiments lies a rawness, the unhealed wounds of those who have suffered in silence. Comment sections overflow with the confessions of souls craving solace.

"Relationships crumble from a single misunderstanding, despite ninety-nine moments of sincerity."

"The Earth is round to remind us not to cry alone in the corners, yet why do we still carve out those corners?"

"Smile, and they say it's fake; cry, and it's exhausting; get angry, and your true self shows; endure, and you become an easy target. What am I supposed to do?"

"After applying courage like an ointment over my wounds, I stick on a bandage called 'challenge,' only to be left with scars named 'success.'"

"Since 1 AM, I've paced on the balcony, thinking of writing a farewell note. As I finish, a sudden thought hits me: I want to laugh at least once before I die."

"Remember when your joke made me laugh? Of course. But have I ever laughed out of happiness?"

"An angel cradled a weeping devil. The devil said, 'Don't hug me... If you do, my bad energy will transfer to you.' The angel smiled and replied, 'Since I've embraced you, I'll share my good energy with you.'"

"Our feet are meant for running, hands for holding, ears for listening, and mouths for speaking. And you? You exist to find happiness. So don't let it dim too much."

"Do you know why gems are precious? Because there are so few in the world. And me? I'm one of a kind in this vast universe too."

We humans know little about one another, and relationships rarely unfold as we wish. We inflict wounds upon each other, sketching our own maps of emotion in the aftermath.

"Human beings are truly complex."

"An father was just another human."

"The truth about my father's coat remains elusive, yet I see he was but a fragile human being."

"I'm sorry for not being a good son." No, I felt regret.

www.ingramcontent.com/pod-product-compliance
Lightning Source LLC
Chambersburg PA
CBHW022129150726
47992CB00002B/508